CU00294868

FRÉDÉRIQUE

FRÉDÉRIQUE:

THE TRUE STORY OF A YOUTH TRANSFORMED INTO A GIRL

DON BRENNUS ALÉRA

DELECTUS

LONDON

1998

First published by Select Bibliothèque Paris, 1921.

This translation published by
Delectus
27 Old Gloucester Street
London
WC1N 3XX

ISBN: 1 897767 08 0

Cover design and additional typesetting
by Image Engineering.

Printed by Woolnough Ltd.,
Irthlingborough, Northamptonshire.

Introduction

Perhaps the world's largest collection of publications from the Select Bibliothèque was held by pioneering sexologist Havelock Ellis. Upon his death the collection was catalogued by Gerschon Legman and passed to the library of The Kinsey Institute for Sex Research in Bloomington, Indiana. Given his personal interests, especially in undinism, it is not surprising that several late Victorian erotic novels including *Gynecocracy* and another Delectus title, *The Petticoat Dominant*, the latter in particular containing similar elements to *Frédérique*, have been wrongly attributed to Ellis by erotic bibliophiles over the years.

It has been suggested by Paul Jerome, in *Dictionnaire des Oeuvres Érotiques*, edited by Pascal Pia (*Paris: Mercure de France 1971*), that the company was run by a man by the name of Massy. He also suggests that the names of the authors were house pseudonyms for a whole stable of writers who produced books for the Select Bibliothèque on such diverse themes such as tight corsets, shoe and glove fetishism, transvestism, rubberwear, enemas, pony girls and women wrestlers!

Don Brennus Aléra, Roland Brévannes and Bernard Valonnes were almost certainly the same person as each name is an anagram of the other, if you take the *u* as a *v* in case of Aléra. Whoever they were, almost sixty of the one hundred or so books published by the Select

Don Brennus Aléra

Frédérique

HISTOIRE VÉRIDIQUE

D'un ADOLESCENT CHANGÉ en FILLE

Que sais-je?

SELECT BIBLIOTHÈQUE
SCEAUX (SEINE)

— 1921 —

The original title page reproduced from the 1921 edition.

Bibliothèque in the early part of this century, from around 1905 until the mid-1930s, carried one of their names as the author. A note by Legman on Album 7, a collection of booksellers and rubber goods catalogues in the British Library, formerly owned by the Marquis of Milford Haven, brother of the late Lord Louis Mountbatten, identifies Roland Brévannes as the real author of the books.

Louis Perceau, in *Bibliographie du Roman Érotique* (Paris: Georges Fourdrinier 1930), reveals that the author also used the name of "Pierrot" for a book entitled *Une Séduction* (1908), which was reprinted several times, and two others *L'Acte Bref* and *L'Art de Jouir ou Traite Pratique des Caresses Voluptueuses, Recettes et Formules sur les Aphrodisiaques et Philtres d'Amour* (1908). The latter book was also subject to a condemnation pronounced by the La cour d'assises de la Seine on 11 October 1913. I also have another book by Aléra from his pre-Select Biliothèque days, *Mémoires d'un Flagellant de Marque: Publiés d'après le journal intime du baron de M...* The book carries the name of Henri Pauwels as publisher and probably dates from around 1906. The book was later published by the Select Bibliothèque in a slightly different form as *Le Tour du Monde d'un Flagellant.*

Further information is given in the original French edition of *Frédérique* which provides a brief biography of Aléra at the rear of the book:

"*Don Brennus Aléra's descriptive style makes his readers feel that he is a precursor in this realm. His deep insight into the human heart, its perverse aberrations and mental and carnal depravities allow him to unveil artificial paradises and salacious underworlds to his readers. His colourful and picturesque style blended with his vivid imagination make the scenes of his creation come to life and the reader can identify with his disconcerting and enigmatic, but also prepossessing characters."*

A biography also appears for Brévannes:

"Roland Brévannes, who is very well-versed in Satanism and the occult, has made several journeys to the Far East and has stopped over in the Indies; thanks to his erudition, he has studied texts divulging the secrets of hermetic science; he has skilfully popularised them with the help of his scintillating style, has made them accessible to all.

Thanks to his experience, his knowledge and the evidence which he has witnessed, he is exceptionally placed to tackle questions which are by no means banal and whose novelty is unparalleled by the powers of the imagination."

Gershon Legman unkindly called him a low hack, in his introduction *The Private Case* by Patrick Kearney (Jay Landesman 1981) when, as you will find, Mr. Aléra's style is opulent and florid. For example, in the sequence when Frédérique is locked in the cupboard with the Baroness's exotic clothes, the dazzling description of his olfactory sensations owe much to the style of J.K. Huysmans in his classic decadent novel *Against Nature*. Understandably, once again, Select Bibliothèque wax lyrical over their own high literary standards:

*"Select Bibliothèque only publishes works of excep-
tional literary merit and interest which address riv-
eting yet unfamiliar topics and which contain hith-
erto unpublished disclosures; those are the criteria
which characterise all our publications, whether
past or forthcoming, and whose indisputable
uniqueness is unrivalled.....Select Bibliothèque publishes material which is ex-mainstream, illustrated
by choice artists and which guarantees our readers an original content as well as an impeccable
style."*

The Memoirs of an Erotic Bookseller by Armand Coppens
(Luxor 1969)* features a scene in which the wife of a
collector, Mrs. Cramming, forces her husband to sell
his collection of forty volumes of The Select Bibliothèque
to Coppens. The collection included the First three volumes in the series, *Fred*, *Frédérique* and *Frida* (coming soon from Delectus). The last two in this series
Fridoline, and *Lina Frido* are incredibly rare and I have
never seen a copy anywhere in my ten years in the business.

The last catalogue observed by myself was issued in
1936, and contained almost 90 titles. The onset of war
sent the presses quiet and no further books appeared
from the Select Bibliothèque.

Michael R. Goss
London 1998

* Pseudonym of Amsterdam bookseller and bibliophile W.N.Schors,
still active now although only in the Occult Sciences.
Note: All translations in the introduction are by Valerie Orpen.

Chapter One

The Aunt and the Nephew

For a few minutes after waking, Fred de Montignac was completely disorientated. Accustomed to the hushed murmurs and merry whispers which signalled the awakening of the dormitory, he did not immediately recognise his surroundings. At first, something felt amiss in the total silence around him; then, as his eyes grew accustomed to the darkness of the room where both shutters and heavy curtains blotted out daylight, he was astonished not to behold the vast rooms where four or five of the best-behaved boarders were grouped together. Each morning, except after one of those nights spent in the dungeon and which still haunted him, he was used to waking up to the presence of pupils of the Sainte-Brigitte boarding-school, their gender made ambiguous by their feminine garments. But today was different: he was alone in a bedroom that was far more elegant and luxurious and where the only bed to be seen was his own.

It all flooded back: he was staying with his aunt, the beautiful, majestic and awe-inspiring Baroness Saint-Genest who, three days earlier, had driven to the heart of the Touraine in her motorcar to collect Fred and bring him back to Paris and to his seriously ailing mother. The joy with which he would normally have greeted this unexpected release after months of captivity, suffering and even torture was countered by his grief. Had he not been so fearful of mishap, he would have been deliriously happy at the mere thought of leaving this hell behind. The slightest reference to that sinister establishment would bring a lump to his throat; a maelstrom of images would dance before his eyes: the classrooms and playgrounds teeming with boarders, some of whom were visibly embarrassed to wear girls' clothes; the curls, the powder, the ladies' gloves, which boys as well as girls were forced to wear; the constant ordeal of constricting corsets which strangled the waist or boots so tightly-laced that the flesh of the calves bulged out of them, and the whole gamut of punishments, some humiliating, others painful, all of them aberrant.[1]

The din of slammed doors, the sound of running feet, screams, calls and sobs drove out these visions and brought the youth back into reality with a thud; his mother was in her death throes and his presence was needed immediately. Death left in its wake a house plunged into turmoil. On the day of the final and dismal ceremony, Fred was struck down by a fever and became ill. The time spent at the terrifying English institution, his hurried return followed by this bereavement which had come like a thunderbolt,

[1] This alludes to the detailed scenes in *Fred* the first volume in the series by the same author (published by Select-Bibliothèque).

it had all been too much for this child's vibrant and excitable nerves. He was sent to his tutor's country retreat where he was ill for a few days, convalesced for a few weeks and finally recovered. He remained with his tutor for six months, recovered from the shock, forgot his nightmarish existence at Sainte-Brigitte and fostered tender memories of his doleful and gentle mother.

One day, his tutor announced that the family council had decided to entrust him to his aunt, the Baroness Saint-Genest who resided in Paris and who would take him in and see to his upbringing. The news was not ill-received by Fred who quivered pleasurably and blushed a little. From an early age, Fred had been sensitive to feminine charm and beauty, to the prettiness of finery, frills and flounces, to the delicacy of luxurious fabrics and had consequently been unconsciously aroused by the lofty splendour and the domineering allure of this blond creature. She was graceful in a smooth and regal manner, she radiated mature sensuality and her innate majesty was exquisitely tempered by enveloping and imperious gestures, a voice at once caressing and commanding, the sparkle of her keen, expressive and darting eyes and two rows of gleaming teeth revealed by the smile of her voluptuously-drawn lips.

When she arrived, she had not changed, she was still distinguished, stately and graceful and he smiled at the bold, proud eyes which peered into his blue irises. He also smiled at her curvaceous and statuesque figure so congruent with the serene beauty of her youthful, smooth features which belied her thirty-five years.

Although he was not able to analyse his feelings, she seemed more desirable and commanding to him than ever in her mourning dress which improved her figure and enhanced the camellia-like paleness of her skin. The woman whom he used to call 'his beautiful aunt' had never seemed so extraordinarily beautiful, and thanks to her charm, her brilliance, her finery and her perfumes, she was akin to a goddess in latterday costume in whose presence he felt secretly flustered. His gaze fondled, so to speak, the harmonious curves of her plenteous hips, of her thighs moulded by her skirt, of her sloping shoulders and her generous breasts which stretched the fabric of her bodice; it travelled over her naked arms, white and pure, plump and dimpled, and finished up into the opulent and proud *décolletage* which revealed the symmetrical undulation of her bosom.

She gazed back at him, but with less contentment; she barely recognised her nephew in this bespoke mourning suit; she detected even less the bygone odd effect produced by the feminine uniform imposed on him at the Stockley establishment; she even gave a hint of a dismayed pout at the sight of his flat-heeled boots and his hair, which, though not exactly short, had nevertheless nothing feminine about it. Fred vaguely divined his aunt's thoughts as he followed her gaze. His suspicions were confirmed when the handsome Léontine observed:

"You seem shorter, Fred."

"Yet my tutor is of the opinion that I have grown."

"It's your shoes that give that impression: those high-heeled boots made you look much taller."

The remark annoyed Fred because it brought back all too strong memories of Sainte-Brigitte.

Soon, he was packed. A new life awaited him. He had been orphaned at the age of fourteen, was to inherit a private income of 15,000 *livres* a year bequeathed to him by his mother and he was about to be entrusted to this aunt who had always displayed an affectionate interest towards him, albeit tinged with bizarre rapture; she was affluent and could afford a comfortable existence: she would provide well for him and would make him materially happy. Fred de Montignac was ready to place his trust and his future into her hands, and yet, standing on the threshold of his unknown destiny, he was inexplicably and profoundly apprehensive.

When Léontine came to fetch him, she looked superb; a becoming hat crowned her magnificent hair and her alabaster arms were sheathed in shimmering black satin gloves.

Just as they were about to get into the car, Madame de Saint-Genest, who was hurrying the boy in front of her as if she were making off with her prey, said, with an enigmatic smile and in a tremulous voice:

"I still think you looked prettier dressed as a girl."

Fred winced in defiance as if his gender was

once again under attack; but he soon regained his composure for her kid-gloved arm coiled itself around his neck, rested on his shoulders as her small, precise hand stroked his cheek affectionately.

Fred's prejudices fell away. He remained silent but once he had sat down against her soft warm hip he enquired:

"I won't ever be sent back to Sainte-Brigitte, will I?"

"Providing you obey me, I will keep you with me; but you will have to obey me in every way."

Her tone was so cryptic that Fred did not reply; but he anxiously and quizzically glanced up at her placid and domineering face. He was astonished and intimidated to see her features hardened by a sudden spark which set her eyes ablaze; for the remainder of the journey, he was silent and dared not look at his aunt.

Chapter Two

The Trials of Dressing

When Fred awoke for the first time in the bedroom which his aunt had allotted to him, he was astounded to discover that all his boys' garments had been removed during his sleep and replaced with girls' clothes. He was overcome with anger, as in his Sainte-Brigitte days, to such an extent that he was still in bed when his aunt sent the chambermaid to enquire about his tardiness.

He told the servant-girl that he would only get out of bed when his boys' clothes had been returned.

Rose reported this answer to the Baroness who, frowning, ordered her to repeat the attempt.

"You must make him understand that I shall not tolerate the slightest resistance; I shall crush him and if he rebels too frequently, I shall have him sent back to Sainte-Brigitte with a special recommendation to the headmistress. This prospect should calm him; I do not think you will have much difficulty in subduing him. You will dress him, even though he is quite capable of dressing himself; it will come in useful whenever he takes it into his head to be refractory; and while you are about it, you can lace his corset and boots as tightly as you possibly can."

The *soubrette* to whom she was giving all these instructions was quick-witted and impudent, a petite, determined and nervous brunette whose sharp and precise gestures testified to her boundless energy.

I can rely on Rose thought Léontine as the chambermaid withdrew. The beautiful widow had no intention of carrying out her threat of sending him back to Sainte-Brigitte. In the past, she had regretted seeing him packed off to that boarding-school; she was now only too glad to have him in her clutches and to bring him up in accordance with her personal views and tastes which were thoroughly bizarre and perverse to say the least. One could sense it from the peculiar expression on her serenely beautiful face or by the languid way in which she would loll on her padded *chaise-longue*, lost in a voluptuous daydream.

Her first reaction had been to get up and personally take this troublesome and irritable child to task; but she had changed her mind: it was best if she did not display her authority against a trivial instance of mutiny; if it was to be a little acrimonious, the first contact with the young rebel was best left to Rose; Léontine could always intervene if the chambermaid remained powerless; then the boy, exhausted after his energetic struggle, would be more manageable.

She nevertheless hoped that Fred, shaped by the regime of the mixed boarding-school, would not put up an unflagging resistance; perhaps Rose was this very minute transforming him into a slender, saucy girl whom she would presently bring in.

The Baroness was mistaken; this would have been possible if she had been able to take in Fred immediately after his leaving school. But the bereavement and the ensuing illness had broken the pattern: the Stockley discipline was now nothing more than an abhorrent memory which no longer held sway over the youth who had forgone those habits instilled by force and had resumed a liking for the clothes and occupations more becoming to his sex.

Léontine was consequently dismayed when Rose returned alone.

"Well, what about Fred?"

"A real little devil! I can't get the better of him; he runs across the room in his shift, he has torn one shift to shreds and broken a chair."

"Could you not hold him down?"

"Quite possibly, provided I had both hands free; as soon as I tried to put on his corset, he managed to slip out, run out of my grasp and I was back to where I began."

"Indeed!... Well you will have to go back and try again; I give you permission to tie his hands behind his back. Use the belt from my purple dressing-gown, that way you can bind him tightly without hurting him. He must give in to you; I really cannot be disturbed every time you encounter some obstacle with him." These last words were uttered a little curtly.

"I'll try again and we shall see," retorted the maid sharply and angrily.

At the barely audible sound of Rose's hand on the doorknob, Fred, who was on the bed, sat up aggressively and looked towards the threshold.

Rose annoyed him because, dressed in a close-fitting dress with a lace collar and cuffs, she reminded him of the teachers at the Stockley boarding-school; he consequently could not help feeling belligerent towards her.

Rose half-opened the door and peered round mischievously. She teased him:

"So, Monsieur Fred, have we calmed down? I see that you have not broken the looking-glass or the dressing-table...There is still hope!"

This banter maddened him and he clenched his fists.

Rose approached him, feigning indifference, with the belt hidden behind her back. When she was close to Fred, who was giving her challenging looks and gestures, she suddenly seized his wrist, knocked him off the bed and took advantage of the momentum to make him stumble forwards a little. He had hardly had time to come to his senses before she had tied the belt around one wrist and grabbed the other arm so as to join both wrists behind his back, tightly locking them together.

Fred hurled abuse at her and stamped his foot but she ignored him; abandoning her powerless captive, she busied herself with gathering all the clothes which were scattered around the room.

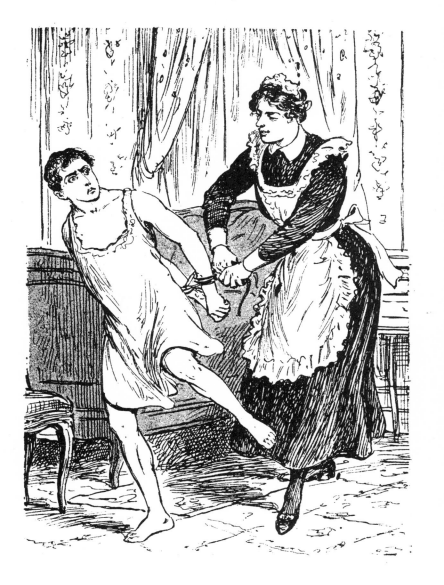

Rose ne se souciait pas de ses invectives (Chap. II).

She succeeded in putting the corset around him and fastening it completely; all that was left now was to lace it up more tightly; the position of the arms was bothersome but not a hindrance and Rose began to pull on the pale silk laces. Fred's contortions did not succeed in foiling the maid's efforts, but by dint of kicking, he managed to delay the proceedings.

Irritated by those blows which she had been unable to dodge, Rose tugged with all her might. As the laces glided through her nimble fingers, so his waist became increasingly slender, moulding the protuberance of his hips and aggravating his discomfort in this supple armour. Léontine's orders were fully carried out and Rose pulled with such enthusiasm that Fred thought that he would choke.

On the strength of this first result, Rose decided to slip a petticoat on him and succeeded; it proved a little arduous but the laces were nevertheless tied at the waist and the boy's thighs were trapped in an imponderable cascade of frills and flounces.

The maid came up against another hurdle when she attempted to slip on the sheer, glossy stockings that had been put aside for him. Fred was stamping his feet with such frenzy that putting on his shoes was quite out of the question.

Just as she was pondering on how to subdue this insolent youth, the Baroness entered the room.

"What? Have you only got this far?"

Her tone was sharp but her expression belied it. She had suddenly softened at the sight of the oddly elegant figure of this Adonis, improved and feminised by the stylish and luxurious lingerie.

In fact, she did not conceal her ecstasy and went up to him, smiled and exclaimed,

"You little devil! How feminine attire suits you! The corset has already completely altered your figure; thanks to that gossamer petticoat, you seem to be stepping out of a giant flower. And that waist!...Oh that waist..., so slender it seems it could snap in two!...I swear my hands could encircle it."

She cheerfully confirmed this by standing in front of her nephew and gripping his wasp-waist in her tapered and perfectly manicured fingers.

Fred recoiled and jerked out of her grasp.

"What is the matter?" asked Léontine sharply, "Are you still behaving like a spoilt child? You will soon resume your sweet temper and good manners when you have donned girls' clothes."

Fred flinched and the two ladies wondered if he was about to scream or cry; finally he stamped his feet in frenzy.

"As Madame can see for herself, Monsieur Fred is insufferable," remarked the maid, "I cannot continue his *toilette*, I would need to tie his ankles together which would make shoeing him impossible."

"I'll hold him down and we shall get the better of him."

Rose pulled up a chair behind Fred and tumbled him on to it while his aunt forced him to remain seated by pressing down on his shoulders; next, Rose knelt down and grabbed a leg to sheath it with

Enervée, Rose serra sans ménagement (Chap. II).

silk. She had placed a pair of tall laced boots within reach; Fred's gaze fell on the heels, delicate Louis heels, narrow, waisted and dizzyingly high.

"No! Not girls' shoes! I shan't wear them!" protested Fred, soundly kicking the maid who fell over backwards.

"Oh it's like that, is it? Rose," ordered the Baroness, "tie this scoundrel to the back of the chair, so that my hands can be free to assist you."

She pressed down nervously onto Fred's shoulders while the maid went off to find some bonds.

When she returned with a bundle of rope, her mistress said, "Perhaps this precaution is superfluous: I feel in the mood to give my nephew a good spanking which will subdue him for a while."

Gripped by Rose's firm hand, the youth was unceremoniously made to stand, then positioned over Léontine's lap after she had sat down to receive him.

She hitched up his petticoat and shift to expose his buttocks. "It's quicker than in the days when you wore trousers," she jested.

She dealt out a few resounding slaps which made his skin blush. She hit fast and with all her might, her rings digging into his young flesh; she must have hurt him for she heard a muffled moan.

She stopped and handed him back to the maid who sat him down and resumed tying him up. Rose tied the rope several times around his abdomen and the chair's crossbars while the boy's hands were still firmly tied together; just to make quite sure, she also strapped one of his legs to the chairleg.

Tightly bound and unable to move, the unruly boy was totally at the two women's mercy.

Madame de Saint-Genest stooped to seize his free leg and lifted it horizontally while Rose pulled on the stocking. The rebellious Fred still tried to struggle; Léontine held the leg more securely, clenching it with both hands, tightening her vice-like grip around it and pressing it against her bosom which Fred could feel, soft and palpitating.

Only then did Rose succeed in slipping on the silky and diaphanous sheath over his long and slender leg, up to mid-thigh, and fastening it to the garter which matched the ribbons of his shift. She then wrapped his foot in a supple fawn-coloured boot which came up to his calf; sitting cross-legged, she laced it up as tightly as possible so that his foot was cast in taut shiny kid.

That leg was then strapped to the chair leg while the other leg was untied and left to the maid's care.

"Well, that's done," uttered the Baroness. "Rose, you will have no trouble in finishing his *toilette*. The lesson has borne its fruit, without a doubt."

Fred mumbled a few unintelligible words.

"What's that I hear, you naughty boy? If Rose can't get the better of you, you will be whipped again."

"No, I shan't: I'm too old for that."

"What cheek! Listen, Fred: I am going to get ready to go out; before I leave the house, I shall

L'indomptable Fred dut renoncer à se débattre (Chap. II).

look in and if you are not yet fully dressed, I swear I shall whip you again!"

Having proffered these words, she raised her naked arm, wagged a threatening finger at him and walked off in a rustle of silk.

Now that Rose was alone with him, she untied the knots and put a shift on him just as she had done with the petticoat. She then admonished him, "Fred, I'm now going to untie your wrists because otherwise I can't put on your bodice. Do you promise to be a good boy?"

Fred did not answer but took advantage of his new-found freedom to circumvent the maid's attempts; she was upset, beseeched him, threatened him and talked of calling the Baroness.

Precious time was thus squandered in words and struggles and when Madame de Saint-Genest returned, Rose was still clutching the bodice and Fred was still naked from the waist up.

Since retiring to her chambers, the Baroness had completely altered her appearance: an elegant hat crowned her mass of wavy hair and long shimmering kid gloves enveloped her ravishing arms. In this outfit, she made on Fred a sudden and violent impression which so perfectly matched her statuesque figure and her haughty beauty.

The youth remained motionless and gazed at his aunt as if for the first time. Rose took advantage of his stillness to grab his wrists.

"What? Still not dressed? You remember what I promised...Rose, make Fred kneel on the easy-chair and hold his hands."

Léontine placed her gloved hand on Fred's naked shoulder, which made him thrill oddly and briefly, and led him to the easy-chair. Fred let himself be guided with a docility which astonished the pair.

"Aunt! Aunt! I beg of you!..." he stammered as he knelt onto the seat while Rose pulled his arms over the back of the chair.

In reply, the Baroness merely advised the maid to firmly hold Fred's wrists. She simultaneously hitched up his shift and petticoat which she held against his shoulder with her left hand while her other hand rained down onto his young bottom.

Fred abandoned all thought of struggling and surrendered with unaccustomed docility and passivity to the mild punishment. Having noticed that Fred had given up the fight, she contented herself with a few stinging though not vindictive smacks. She had no inkling of what was going on in Fred's mind and he would have been unable to define it; but from the moment that supple and fragrant glove had come into contact with his naked shoulder, he had felt his resistance subside; although this spanking was shorter and less violent than the first, it was more effective. Not because of the pain, of which Fred was barely aware, nor because of the humiliation, given that he was now resigned and no longer ashamed to be punished, rather, it was something indefinable which stemmed from the sensation of the gloved hand — that same hand which had hurt him earlier — against his naked skin, something resembling a brutal caress and which wormed itself inside him, destroying his willpower and subjecting him to this beautiful and regal woman's wishes.

As she was leaving, Léontine turned round:

"Of course, an outing with me is out of the question today; you will stay here and as for you, Rose, if he becomes unbearable, you will follow my instructions and leave him there until my return."

And she left without being more explicit.

Rose added the finishing touch to Fred's dress, namely the bodice; she included a few ribbons and dotted a few pins here and there. Fred complied; he was still under Léontine's spell, but it was slowly fading. When the chambermaid led him to a mirror to show him his unexpected and transformed aspect, he was seized by another fit of rage; he threatened to tear his detested clothes to shreds and his demeanour indicated that he would put this to action.

Rose barely had time to snatch his wrists; he wriggled like a worm and kicked out at random; she knew that she would wear herself out and let him escape; so she joined his arms behind his back, tied them firmly and led him to the dressing-room where the Baroness kept all her frocks.

"Those are your aunt's orders!" Rose declared tersely in reply to his protests.

Chapter Three

The Perfumed Prison

Rose opened the door, pushed Fred inside and locked him in.

This wardrobe was no ordinary cupboard; it was a sort of narrow corridor fitted out to accommodate frocks and coats and lined with shelves for hats and shoes. It was totally dark.

Fred was very scared of the dark; this natural fear had been aggravated by his memories of the dungeons at Sainte-Brigitte. Finding himself abruptly plunged into darkness, he was seized by panic which rendered him dumbstruck and rigid with terror; the discomfort incurred by the bonds around his arms rekindled the more unpleasant recollections of the long hours spent in confinement; he was paralysed with fear.

Yet, amid this silence, this darkness and this stillness so complete that he felt as if his senses had been snatched away from him, one sensation overtook all others; he felt surrounded, bathed, penetrated, almost borne by a perfumed aura. Never before had he been thus immersed in a haze of varied and penetrating scents which wafted from all those women's clothes. His only remaining sense was olfactory; he existed solely through his dilated nostrils filled with pervasive fragrances. He was overwhelmed, buoyed up by a haze composed of scents so intense, so alive and complex as to make up something more tangible and more substantial than a mere atmosphere. Rather, it was an ocean of perfumed waves assailing him relentlessly as if he were a rock endlessly beaten by the breakers.

Every conceivable scent could be detected among these perfumed waves which steeped him in a strange sensual delight: the smell of luxurious fabrics, whiffs of face-powder and expensive oils, the strong, musky odour of furs and, intermingled with this symphony, an arousing and heady scent of woman. All these fragrances, strong or subtle, distinct or imprecise, stirred his nerves and his brain, sent sensual shivers through his entire frame, penetrated his flesh and aroused a strange flurry which heralded untold pleasures at the core of his virginal being, Fred, intoxicated and whisked away into a mysterious paradise, yielded to its power.

Little by little, his daze gave way to rational thoughts; he wanted to be conscious of these numerous sensations, to compare and define them: he moved around, taking small steps, caressed by fabrics that were like the quivering wings of a bird of paradise. Because he could not move his hands tied behind his back, he spread his fingers in an attempt to clutch a fold of velvet, a silk flounce, a ribbon or a fragment of lace. But his face tried to discover more than his bound hands: he buried his face at random in the invisible and weightless jumble which took shape by its *frou-frou* and its smell. His cheeks and his forehead were caressed by gossamer lawn, impalpable gauze, rustling satin, soft silk and velvet so pleasing to the touch. His nostrils passionately inhaled these hovering scents.

He even sought them out at the heart of the bodices and skirts, rummaging avidly with his nose among the tiers of flounces and the overhanging layers of lace; he discovered smells specific to this or that material saturated with the vestiges of the Baroness' perfumes as well as the feminine fragrance of her warm armpits or her well-groomed skin, anointed with unguents, lotions, rouge and smoothed by fine powder.

He could detect these clues especially when he thrust his head into the necklines of her bodices or where the sleeves widened out; and so he continued his exploration, encountering supple cloth after crisp satin, stiff moire after limp silk. On occasion, deep in a fold, he would happen across a fragrant sachet whose bouquet went to his head; then he would stumble across something at once resistant and soft, or a wild smell mitigated by something very pervasive and refined which bore all the hallmarks of a fur coat.

Having reached the far end of the closet, he upset a box which protruded from a shelf; he knelt down to find out what it contained and, using his cheeks and his lips, discovered cool, supple and scented objects which could only be gloves.

Sprawled on the floor, he rubbed his face with sheer delight against the *glacé* kid and the velvety suede which his lips recognised with growing rapture; he stood up again to press himself against the silk, brush against the tulle, kiss the lace and bite into the fur, with such fervour that, intoxicated by the feather-like caresses and made tipsy by the subtle and insidious scents, he eventually fell to his knees and collapsed onto the parquet floor, slowly and deliciously losing consciousness, overcome by a perfumed dream.

Rose, astonished by his silence, cautiously opened the closet door. For a moment, she was very alarmed to see him sprawled lifelessly on the floor and her first impulse was to untie his hands; but as soon as she did so, she realised that he was simply fast asleep and blissfully happy and smiling; she had some trouble rousing him.

She had only just awoken him when Madame de Saint-Genest returned. She asked about her nephew's conduct as soon as she entered the hall.

"Monsieur Fred has behaved odiously, he threatened to tear what he was wearing, to break everything in the room so I was obliged to obey Madame's orders and lock him in the closet where he fell asleep."

"Send him to my room immediately."

The chambermaid led the youth to the threshold of the room which Léontine had just entered. She had not yet removed her hat or gloves and scornfully gave her nephew the briefest of looks over her shoulder, then ensconced herself majestically in an imposing easy-chair; sitting comfortably, she leaned on the armrest and crossed her legs, one knee over the other, revealing a long, round and shapely leg with a slender ankle sheathed in shimmering silk and shod in a disconcertingly arched and brazenly stiletto-heeled boot.

She scrutinised Fred and sized him up.

"So once again you are dressed as a girl! We've achieved it at long last...You really are an ill-natured boy!"

As she spoke, she unthinkingly dangled her foot and the supple kid, thin and taut like a glove, shimmered and mesmerized Fred.

She noticed how deeply entranced he was and wondered if he was listening to her:

"Come now, Fred! Look at me and answer me."

When he had lifted his gaze towards her calm and proud face which had suddenly become stern, she pursued,

"Don't take it for granted that I'll put up with your tantrums. I know full well that you won't become docile overnight but I am convinced that those clothes will play a part in your metamorphosis; from now on, those girls' clothes are here to stay, it's useless trying to rebel."

She had anticipated protests but was mistaken and so continued,

"Have you lost your tongue? Perhaps you have finally understood that you are far more becoming now than when you were a boy. Your blue eyes and your fair complexion are perfectly in tune with this feminine attire and your stay at Mrs. Stockley's taught you how to wear these garments with an ease which may soon develop into elegance. So that's settled: you will keep them on and I hope Rose's only intervention will be to lace or hook you up, add a pin here or a ribbon there, in short, her only duty will be to assist you in your *toilette* and to instil stylishness in you. Do you promise to be well-behaved?"

An affirmative grunt, exclaimed in one breath, was his sole reply.

"No, no!" exclaimed the beautiful Léontine, "I demand a clearer answer, a formal commitment, almost a pledge. I want you to swear that you will keep on your girls' clothes. In any case, it makes sense, given that you will henceforth be called Frédérique, Fré-dé-ri-que."[2]

"But my name is Frédéric and everybody calls me Fred!"

"Oh, but that was long ago, when everybody thought you were a boy, before you entered Sainte-Brigitte. Come now, Frédérique, my dear, to begin with, I want you to apologise for your earlier conduct."

"Please forgive me, aunt."

"No, not like that! After such a tantrum, you will have to implore my forgiveness on your knees."

Fred moved closer to the Baroness who was pointing an imperious finger at the carpet. As he

[2] In French, 'Frédérique' is the feminine version of 'Frédéric' and their pronunciation is ambiguously identical (translator's note).

Il faut me jurer autre chose aussi... (Chap. III).

approached her, he could discern exquisite fragrances redolent of the arousing perfumes which still intoxicated him. Léontine had just handled her fine cambric handkerchief and the essence with which it was saturated wafted over towards Fred.

"Very well, I forgive you," she said.

He seized the hand that was closest to his lips, slender, distinct and encased in the long, black glove which reached above the elbow. He could distinctly perceive the pervasive smell, at once a little wild and delicate, which emanated from that statuesque arm and that heavenly hand and which sharply contrasted with the invisible, scented haze which encircled this blond goddess; when his lips touched the supple and shiny sheath, he thought he would faint and prolonged his pious and submissive kiss.

A contented smile softened Léontine's haughty features and, in a domineering and coaxing tone, she said,

"You accept to be dressed as a girl; your name is Frédérique de Montignac and you promise to obey me unconditionally."

With strange fervour, he made the requested pledge and stooped even lower to underscore his subservience with a kiss on the gleaming boot close to his face.

This homage pleased the aunt no end and sparked off profound emotions in her nephew; the memory of the recent sensations experienced in the perfumed prison flooded back with extraordinary clarity, he was totally captivated by the magic of female regalia, so fragrant, delicate and opulent with its silk stockings, kid boots, *glacé* kid gloves, satin gowns and diaphanous lingerie. Madame de Saint-Genest, who had pre-empted his feelings, took advantage of them to put the finishing touches to her authority and bend him to her innermost wishes. Placing her black-gloved hand onto his light-brown curls, she pressed his child's head further onto her boot. Fred surrendered and covered the boot with kisses, whose warmth and passion she could feel through the expensive leather.

In a voice altered by an ambiguous arousal and smug satisfaction, she slowly added,

"You must swear one final thing: never to cut your hair. It is too short; it must grow so that I can style it as I please; it would be a sin to wield the scissors on it."

While he stammered another pledge interspersed with kisses, she rapped out,

"You will be dressed as a girl!...You will let your hair grow!...Your name will be Frédérique!..."

She sensed that her influence had permeated his very soul and that her will was beginning to taint his.

Chapter Four

Under the Spell of the Sorceress

That very evening, Madame de Saint-Genest applied herself to fashioning him according to her whims, to mould this young being, who was not exactly a boy any more, like clay. She intended to transmogrify him completely, to transform him into an accomplished young lady whose sex would never be called into question. Relinquishing all the trappings of masculinity was not enough; she strove to surround him with an exclusively feminine environment by taking every opportunity to make him behave, live and even think like a girl.

With this goal in mind, she paid meticulous attention to detail. Fred — or rather Frédérique as she now called him without fail — was transferred to a bright bedroom, daintily furnished, hung with immaculate drapes and crammed with tasteful bric-à-brac. Vases of blooming flowers were ever present; the wardrobe was filled with piles of sumptuous lingerie in which little perfumed sachets were buried; the mirrors reflected each other's gleam; a delicate fragrance wafted through the room; the dressing-table was laden with bottles, powder puffs and manicure implements; the bookshelves contained every young lady's favourite tomes.

By gratifying Frédérique with the most expensive and stylish lingerie and shoes, by showering him with lace, ribbons and furbelows, Léontine was intent on developing a taste in feminine finery in her nephew. This penchant was already innate in him regarding the accessories which Madame de Saint-Genest used to enhance her proud and cool grace; he now needed to be encouraged to consider with equal interest the clothes and accessories which were an integral part of his own wardrobe or which complemented it.

This taste, which had manifested itself briefly and intermittently when Fred had been a boarder at Mrs. Stockley's, had become more positive during his adoring confinement which he had endured in the closet amongst the coats, frocks, bodices, petticoats and scarves whose folds concealed such titillating mysteries and such feminine fascination. As soon as the youth had become accustomed to the discomfort of tapering high heels and tightly-laced corsets, he began to experience the pleasure of feeling imponderable lawn and cambric against his skin softened by creams and perfumed with essences; the caresses of silk, satin and velvet became agreeable when they came into contact with his own body and he sometimes lingered in front of the tall mirror, lost in a satisfied contemplation of his waist slimmed by the corset, his rounded hips, his naked arms and his elegant figure emerging from the gauzy waves of the most stylish frills.

A deep-seated rebellion would sometimes well up in him but it would be countered by the memory of the promise which he had made to his beautiful aunt and he would resume the pleasurable occupation of donning all his finery to please Léontine. In so doing, elegance and luxury unwittingly became second nature to him and supplanted his boyish instincts and inclinations.

In any case, the Baroness kept him under close scrutiny, being aware of the influence of her presence and the magnetic power of her touch. As soon as she anticipated a glimmer of resistance on his part, she would annihilate it before it had had time to develop, and this with a mere look, smile or gesture, by pointing her arched foot shod in an imperious boot or by placing her commanding hand, so perfect and aristocratic in its expensive glove, on his naked arm or his uncovered nape.

She often attended her nephew's *toilette* and thus acquainted him with the daily routine of the most refined coquettishness; under the Baroness's guidance, Rose was made to wait upon Fred, and initiated him early on to all the rituals and mysteries of a lady's dressing-room.

Thus, from the moment he awoke, Fred was steeped in a specific environment; all these exterior things were taking effect on him right down to his bedtime, with a force and relentlessness which were sure to yield results. After the first week, his appearance was profoundly altered; careful grooming had brought his body into harmony with his clothes; the fine fabrics and elegantly cut dresses no longer seemed incongruous on this androgynous child who, thanks to his radiant complexion, well-groomed skin and manicured nails, could now compete with the most coquettish girls.

The transformation seemed more radical than it had ever been at Sainte-Brigitte where boys in girls' clothing were made to mix with girls from whom they felt worlds apart. They harboured remnants of roughness and daring, and gestures and bearing seemed contrived. Sometimes the assistant-teacher's supervision would slacken or their desire to impress a *bona fide* girl would make them neglect the imposed affectations and their repressed instinct would resurface; at that juncture, a *je-ne-sais-quoi* would reveal masculinity despite the care taken to conceal gender differences between pupils, and the coquettish frippery would suddenly take on the appearance of a disguise, of fancy-dress worn with ease but which sometimes betrayed its artificiality.

Circumstances like these did not occur in the calm and orderly existence of the old, silent and secluded mansion which served as a palace to one of the most majestic and aristocratic beauties of the faubourg Saint-Germain. There was no vast playground to encourage youthful frolicking, no gaggle of obstreperous children living in fear of the iron rule and always ready to take their revenge on the straitjacket of strict and harshly enforced rules. Fred's only company was the well-mannered and lofty Baroness and her well-trained chambermaid; the former was governed by a passion that was painstakingly kept secret and the latter submitted unthinkingly and zealously to the whims of her employer. As such, there was nothing to rekindle Fred's memory of his real sex; on the contrary, it seemed increasingly clear to him that he could be nothing else but a girl given that he wore girls' clothes, bore a girl's name and led a girl's existence. He was even happy to give in to his aunt's whim insofar as he did not perceive it as an imposition; during those months spent at Sainte-Brigitte, that feeling had been constant, uninterrupted; a fear fuelled by blows, chains and dungeons. Fred had felt like a prisoner at the mercy of his torturers in petticoats, forever brandishing whips or riding-crops, he had felt tamed because he had no other choice, but had continued to rebel in bursts and to aspire to freedom.

It was different now: admittedly, his first confrontation with Rose had been rough and, in order to make him obey, rope and spankings had been resorted to. But at the time, this was to force him to don girls' clothes. Now that this result had been obtained, strong-arm methods had been waived; Fred had forgotten the early struggles; once he had reverted to the garments of the fair sex, a new disposition had presided over his existence, the same artificial disposition which Sainte-Brigitte had instilled in him in a brutal but effective manner; this boarding-school was still fresh in his memory, time had not yet erased Mrs. Stockley's stamp and by donning again corsets, boots and petticoats, Fred had rediscovered, via the undeniable influence of dress, the tendencies with which had been forcibly inculcated and the inclinations which had imperceptibly fermented in him.

Though not as noticeable, Madame de Saint-Genest's authority was greater than Mrs. Stockley's; yet again, he was under a woman's domination, but instead of being a prisoner bound by hempen rope or steel fetters, he was a captive in chains made of flowers.

While Fred was not wholly conscious of his subjection, the Baroness, on the other hand, was acutely aware of her power. When he had knelt before her for an apology which had turned into an homage, she had felt him give himself up and the anticipation of her dearest wish becoming true had caused her heart to leap with joy.

The Baroness had always harboured a vague but obsessional desire which she could not quite analyse; she wanted to be worshipped and adored; she was convinced that the position of mistress waited upon by a slave was the sweetest and most pleasant thing in the world, but she was undecided regarding her slave's sex: on the one hand, she wished to rule over a man so as to gain the satisfaction of imposing her will on the stronger sex, but on the other hand, she would have preferred to be waited upon by a woman for the pleasure of being surrounded by a graceful presence, someone who would move gently and harmoniously and who would be attentive and considerate, something men do clumsily or not at all; insofar as these two options seemed incompatible, she did not attempt to delve deeper into her feelings and her dream remained a vague chimera.

Purely by accident, she had witnessed Fred, dressed for the first time as a girl, being punished for something or another, and this[3] had aroused her secret, darker side; everything seemed crystal clear and the scene had been a revelation to her. It had suddenly dawned on her that she had found a way of fulfilling her fantasy; her tantalized mind and her vivid imagination had conjured up the outline of a plan which was soon thwarted by Fred's admission to Sainte-Brigitte.

But now, it was as if no time had elapsed; Fred was in her power, at her mercy; he had no other relatives to whom he could turn; as it was, he already belonged to her and it would not be long before he became her creature. She had him in the palm of her hand. She had laid the foundations of a daring enterprise nurtured over a long period of time and which she undertook with the resolution to carry it through to the end. She saw nothing quixotic about her concept whose outcome would be the transformation of this young boy into a female slave.

Her plan was two-fold: Fred had to be made effeminate and subjugated, those were her priorities. The transformation had to be implemented before his age ruled it out, artificial tastes had to be instilled and developed so that they became second nature; the enslavement would follow, imperceptible, and concomitant to taking up new habits, so that one day, it would be virtually

[3] This alludes to a scene at the beginning of *Fred* (by the same author and published by Select-Bibliothèque).

achieved and little would be needed to make it complete, absolute and final. Only then would Fred be a thing of the past, and superseded by Frédérique; he would no longer be a boisterous boy, but a composed young lady; the docile and deferential nephew would become a submissive slave complete with the clothes, bearing, gestures, language, tastes, thoughts and even the soul of a girl.

Such was the metamorphosis which the stately blond sorceress had pledged to bring about.

She had embarked on this task with all her heart, eager to overthrow nature by turning a boy into a woman. She was encouraged by the belief that such a thing was feasible and this thought brought a proud and perverse smile to her full lips when she dreamily and regally supervised the chambermaid's feminisation of Fred. Her eyes would light up when she noticed, from day to day, how effeminate he was becoming.

The corset changed his figure, the shoes altered his gait, his movements became more leisurely and flowing, his features more refined and a glimmer of flirtatiousness appeared at the corner of his delicate blue eyes or his fresh, curved lips. Léontine greeted this evidence with sweet rapture for it bolstered her faith in the ultimate success.

No-one could suspect the thoughts which stirred beneath her blond curls when she sat, propped up on one elbow in her usual pose, and covetously watched the youth left to the maid's expertise. But the turmoil in her heart and her strange hopes were betrayed by the triumphant and perverse glint in her beautiful and expressive eyes which would suddenly come alive with a mysterious and unnerving gleam.

Chapter Five

The Stages of a Metamorphosis

Madame de Saint-Genest spent the next few days getting Fred completely used to his girls' clothes and making him wear them outdoors. The youth now felt comfortable with his clothes provided he remained in the luxurious interior of the mansion or in the garden with its ancient trees which was like an oasis sandwiched between grey-walled neighbouring gardens. When his aunt announced that they were to go out together, he felt embarrassed without quite knowing why.

To parade himself outdoors clad in this feminine attire, to walk among strangers who were sure to stare at him with curiosity, to pass boys who would be dressed differently and who would not suspect a hoax, to brush past little girls whom he would outwardly resemble though without ceasing to feel different...all this made him vaguely uneasy.

The Baroness forestalled his unease by nipping it in the bud; as soon as she detected the slightest shadow passing over his lively features, she rang for Rose and ordered her to dress Mademoiselle for a walk, whereupon the chambermaid immediately seized him, removed his shoes and replaced them with boots that were taller, more luxurious, arched and extravagantly-heeled than the last; with her customary deftness, Rose put another frock, a coat and a hat on him and a pair of gloves which she helped him to adjust and button up. Fred was ready before he knew it.

Moreover, Léontine had planned to gradually increase his outings. This first occasion was to be a drive in her motor car. Fred did not, therefore, feel as embarrassed as he had feared; nobody took notice of him; many heads turned towards his aunt, this magnificent woman whose elegance, pulchritude and, especially, majestic placidity caused a sensation everywhere she went. Sometimes people would gaze at him, but in an absent-minded and mechanical way, without insistence.

Consequently, Fred did not feel apprehensive when, two days later, his aunt announced that they were going for a walk. She took him to the Champs-Elysées where a few strollers scrutinised the tall girl accompanying Madame de Saint-Genest a little longer than was necessary; a few must have sensed something peculiar which they could not pinpoint, but they did not attempt to pry more closely into the matter and nothing in their demeanour suggested that their suspicions had been aroused.

Madame de Saint-Genest discreetly observed the impression made by her nephew's disguise; she could not possibly keep him shut away in her mansion; if her future plans were to come to fruition, it was of crucial importance that the transformation should be sufficiently thorough to enable the child to go anywhere unnoticed. This first trial gave her a glimmer of hope in that respect.

But for the time being, it was more Fred's bashful expression which was liable to attract attention. The child felt far more hot and bothered now than during his first outing. Seeing other boys sparked off memories of bygone days when he too sported short trousers, a small jacket or a loose-fitting smock, and he gazed at passing girls in a strained way, telling himself that he now looked like them, and yet...

Léontine's education programme was far too recent to quell Nature; the results which had been obtained so far hinted at the possibility of obtaining other, more radical ones. Madame de Saint-Genest was perfectly aware of this and so did not feel in the least disheartened by her experiment.

She nevertheless thought it preferable not to prolong it further. She was vexed to notice a gleam in Fred's eyes whenever they met a forward little boy with naked legs and a big white collar covering his shoulders; she also noticed that her nephew would suddenly blush and pout regretfully, turning down the corners of his pretty mouth, and she understood that her influence had not yet taken root. A more thorough examination would have bared all and a sharp-eyed observer would have seen through the hoax.

However, the passers-by only had eyes for her; her radiant beauty, her superb figure, her calm and regal bearing drew gazes like a magnet.

Yet, one gentleman considered Fred, stopped and looked round. Had he been older, she would have thought that he was drawn to the vitality of young flesh; but he was young and she could read his suspicions in his sharp eyes.

The incident convinced Léontine and a few minutes later, she hailed a cab and gave the driver her address.

That evening at dinner, she scrutinised Fred/ Frédérique, as she already designated him in her thoughts. He behaved like a girl, he was precociously distinguished, he ate with ease and grace; his face was pretty, youthful and delicately oval-shaped with velvety skin and a ravishingly-shaped mouth. Yet, she had to concede that, although her nephew was an exquisite boy and feminine clothing became him wonderfully, he was not yet a girl.

"What does this pretty face require to feminise it completely?" she wondered. "First of all, it lacks long hair, there's no doubt about that; but that will come in due course...hairpieces can be used as soon as his hair is long enough to be styled; as for a transformation, that would be too obvious and therefore out of the question. Whereas earrings ...yes, earrings ...Now *that* would alter his face and feminise it. And it can be done in an instant, whenever I decide, in three days' time, *she* could have pierced ears."

Léontine had chosen this three-day deadline because she thought it sufficient to prepare Fred. She wished to avoid triggering off one of his tantrums which had formerly proved so violent in this unruly boy; she was always afraid of a revolt, in the wake of a particularly violent outburst, which would undermine her prestige and would cause her to lose her ascendancy which was all too recent to be impregnable. Three days were a minimum to prepare the child for an operation which, all things considered, would be unpleasant, if not painful.

On second thoughts, she wondered if it was necessary to warn him, if it wasn't better to act on the spur of the moment. She would take him to a jeweller's where the piercing would be expertly performed; Frédérique would be effectively mastered, assuming, that is, that the child would even attempt a tantrum in a public place, in the hands and under the gaze of strangers, not only shop assistants, but also customers.

As such, the operation could be over as early as tomorrow.

Tomorrow!...The very idea thrilled Léontine. Since she had made up her mind about this ear-piercing, she had felt increasingly impatient, a feeling which she did not even try to repress. The bizarre passion which motivated the desired metamorphosis had aroused in her a strange and sophisticated sadism which had gradually become the central drive of her existence.

She consequently made up her mind with passionate ecstasy and repeated to herself, "Tomorrow!... It will happen tomorrow!...It is to be tomorrow!"

On the morrow, Fred was dressed as usual, his hair done, his shoes and gloves chosen by Rose with a view to going out. The aunt and the nephew got into a cab and finally alighted outside a jeweller's shop.

Having cast a glance at the twinkling window display, Madame de Saint-Genest entered with an unwary Fred close on her heels.

"Show me your range of earrings!" she ordered, "I have not quite made up my mind yet and I need to see a selection of designs."

The shop assistant opened a few caskets and spread out the jewels. The Baroness had him put by several pairs: hoops, pearls, coloured gems and jet pendants.

Fred looked on absent-mindedly, thinking that she was choosing a jewel for herself or for a friend; he was more engrossed in the comings and goings in the shop, the gesticulations of women who would stop in front of mirrors or point to a coveted jewel. Then he would return to his aunt, unconsciously drawn to the sparkling gems and the gold which the Baroness handled gracefully with her tapered fingers, encased in the supple leather of her expensive gloves, which were made to measure by the very best Parisian *gantier.*

Finally, Madame de Saint-Genest delicately picked up a pair and, smiling, held them up against his childlike face, swinging them beneath his pink lobes.

"I was not mistaken," she said, "these will suit you perfectly. Do you not think, Monsieur, that they make all the difference and make her look prettier?" she asked the assistant.

The assistant approved and paid a few compliments but no-one heard him, Léontine because she was gazing lovingly at his young face with its velvety skin which set off the gems so well, and Fred because he was bewitched by the proximity of her statuesque arm and the touch of her gloved hand.

Once again, her pure and noble features lit up with that same strange expression: her eyes gleamed more than usual and were fixed; her lips curled into a voluptuous smile and her entire body thrilled slightly; her face was aglow with ecstasy, even the white of her teeth seemed more brilliant than usual and there was something deeply disturbing in the sudden change incurred by the passion which had taken hold of her.

As for Fred, he was in a trance; nothing seemed to exist aside from these magnificent arms tightly wrapped in the *glacé* kid sheath whose sheen mesmerized him. He quivered pleasurably when the fine kid brushed against his cheek and ear and his nostrils dilated ecstatically to welcome the delicate female scent combined with the slightly wild and musky smell of the gloves.

Fred had consequently paid no attention whatsoever to his aunt's remark and did not immediately grasp the import of the ensuing conversation between her and the assistant:

"I will take these as well; but you will have to put these on her."

"That should be feasible."

"Her ears are not pierced, can I leave that to you?"

"Certainly."

"Can it be done straight away?"

"As you wish, Madame."

She led Fred into the back room where, the spell having been broken, the youth frowned and recoiled.

"Sit on this chair," ordered Léontine, "and don't fidget."

Fred's gaze followed the jeweller's every move; only when he saw him heating a needle over a flame did those words finally sink in.

"No!" he muttered between clenched and chattering teeth, "No! I shan't have it!"

"Frédérique!" uttered Léontine distinctly, looking him in the eye.

He held her gaze and reiterated his refusal. She paid no heed and forced him to remain seated and said to the assistant,

"Please be quick, Monsieur, I'll hold her down."

But Fred dug in his heels; she saw him blanch with anger, she felt that he was about to clench his fists and stamp his feet but the presence of this stranger and others who had just entered the shop deterred him from doing so. Madame de Saint-Genest entreated the assistant to hurry.

"My niece is a little nervous; the sooner it's over, the better."

She pressed down on Fred's shoulder and pinched his arm. When the man approached, Fred leapt to his feet. The assistant stopped in his tracks and waited.

— Permettez-moi, Madame, d'essayer de la persuasion (Ch. V).

When the child had calmed down a little and had resumed his seat, the jeweller tried again; Fred pushed him away in a rough and brisk manner which was by no means feminine.

"If Mademoiselle refuses to cooperate, we won't get anywhere."

Fred was determined to get his way; the shop assistant hesitated; Léontine was offended and pursed her lips; she spoke *sotto voce* to Fred, punctuating her threat with an emphatic look and an Olympian frown.

Fred glanced at the customers in the shop, thinking that his aunt would shrink from a scene; and, stubbornly shaking his head, he repeated, "I said NO! No! No! And that's final!"

Madame de Saint-Genest grabbed his head between both hands and begged the jeweller to make haste. As Fred was still trying to free himself, the man informed her that he ran the risk of hurting the patient; an erratic gesture could cause facial injuries.

"Don't worry, I'm holding her securely; we could even tie her up if necessary."

"May I try persuading her, Madame?"

Using suave words and a winning smile, he tried to convince the child that it wasn't as dreadful as it seemed. First of all, it would be over very quickly, just a little prick of this gold needle. Was she really that squeamish? If that was the case, he could anaesthetise the lobe with ethyl chloride, it would be superfluous but if that was what she wanted, someone could be sent to the chemist next door; in these conditions, thanks to the cold sensation which would momentarily desensitise the lobe, she would feel nothing, absolutely nothing. Was that not enough to put her mind at rest?...Well, what then? Was she afraid of the sight of blood? But she wouldn't even see it! Even if there was a tiny drop the size of a pinhead, it would immediately be absorbed by the cotton wool!

"And it's all over in a trice!" he concluded, "I could have done it ten times over by now! Would you like me to tie the earrings to your lobes with ribbon so that you can see how pretty you look in a mirror? I'm sure your vanity will persuade you. Smile, now! Do you agree to it?"

But Fred was by no means smiling. He had been afraid of the pain at first; but now it was something else: he was loth to wear these women's ornaments for he was dimly aware that, in order to impose them on him, he was going to be mutilated, albeit slightly, but visibly and durably.

The assistant insisted:

"Is it the proverb which scares you: 'a little pain is necessary to be beautiful'? But it doesn't apply here; I'll take all the necessary precautions to ensure that you do not feel the slightest pain. The most arduous task is to calm your young nerves and overcome your fear! Make a little effort and leave the rest to me."

Fred clung to his latest thought: to refuse to be disfigured. It had never been done to him yet and it was now being forced upon him; they wanted to perforate those earlobes which remain intact in boys but not in girls.

However, given a little more time, perhaps the wilful Fred would have surrendered to the sensuous touch of those gloved hands which clutched his chin, his cheeks, his temples and his hair and which pressed his head against her firm bosom and its palpitating heart. His burst of insubordination must have been very strong to break the spell of this close embrace which was as sweet and fragrant as a caress; perhaps, eventually...

But it was not to be that day, for the jeweller declared, "I give up, Madame. I think it best to postpone the operation to another day, when the young lady has got accustomed to the idea and understands that her fears are unfounded."

Fred breathed a sigh of relief; as he followed his aunt out of the shop, he thought to himself, "It's a reprieve until next time when...well, when exactly the same thing will happen!"

Chapter Six

Awaiting the Fateful Hour

During the ride home, Léontine and Fred remained silent for the most part. To punish him for being disobedient, the Baroness had not permitted him to sit next to her; she had made him sit facing her and had expressed herself in such a way that he came to consider this disgrace as a humiliation.

"In that way," she had told him, "nobody would ever dream that you are my niece, people will think that you are my chambermaid's or my cook's daughter, and you deserve no better."

He had blushed and had fallen silent. A little later, to probe him, she had said, "Why such stubbornness? My orders are always obeyed in the end; do you really want to be punished?"

"I was afraid of the pain."

"You wouldn't have felt a thing, the jeweller told you so."

"And then I thought how it would last forever, how it would always be visible and I didn't want that."

He said nothing more, but this remark made Léontine ponder. That evening, she entered Fred's room, sat next to his bed, lost in a *rêverie* and watched him sleep. She was not contemplating the unadulterated oval shape of his face or his fine features or even the delicate hues of his flesh. No, she was gazing at his ear.

And all the while, she told herself, "nothing is as distinctive as a woman's ear; between the ears of a man and those of a woman, there is a huge and essential difference: women's ears are pierced!"

She recalled Fred's screams of defiance and dwelt upon them.

Yes, she mused, he is aware of it, albeit vaguely. He understands that pierced ears are the final touch to his effeminacy. His transformation will no longer be superficial, but will penetrate his very flesh. Clothes can be removed (she glanced at the chair where Fred had laid his clothes before retiring to bed), they can be removed and while they remain on a chair, what is left of that feminine appearance which I've strived so hard to perfect? Conversely, ear-piercing leaves an indelible mark, a scar which is branded into the flesh. It's a mark, my mark, the sign of my possession, the evidence of my rule over him! I will make a girl of him and that girl will belong to me and will bear the hallmark of her enslavement. I have to be the one who pierces those ears! We shall not return to the jeweller's; perhaps it is all for the best that the operation did not succeed there, it will be performed here instead. We shan't be disturbed; I shall have all the time in the world, all my amenities and Rose will be there to help me. Oh, we shall succeed, even if we have to tie him up! I'll find a way, even if it means hurting him more than usual...

This final thought made her eyes light up and a perverse smile, a shade sadistic, flickered mysteriously over her indolent and imperial face. For she suddenly wondered, with utter clarity,

And why should I avoid hurting him? On the contrary, is it not more desirable that he should suffer at my hands to receive my mark, the one I have decided to brand into him, the one that he will bear eternally, more permanent even than a fetter or a yoke? I now understand that if this slight transformation is to bear its fruit, if this symbol is to be totally meaningful, it must be carried out by force and must involve pain. Rather than curtail the operation, I will do the utmost to eke it out, and given that it is harmless, I shall ensure it is as painful as possible. I shall turn it into a miniature version of the rack. He must never forget, should he live a hundred years, the moment when I branded him in my own way, when he was compelled to sign in blood and tears the pact which made him mine, my very own female slave!

And with feverish eyes and lips curled into a cruel smile, the Baroness developed her idea.

I shall go against the grain of past attempts: instead of winning him over and assuaging his fears, I shall make him more terrified still, I shall exacerbate his squeamishness. I shall do everything in my power to make him resist the operation with all his might. Then, on the crucial day, I shall assemble all the preparations so as to make his imagination run riot; it will be a ceremony, one that is at once painful and mystical. I shall create such a ritual that every single detail will be eternally branded in his memory.

Madame de Saint-Genest's plans were inflexible but not malicious. She would not have wished to inflict unnecessary pain on Fred of whom she was sincerely fond in her own special way. She was simply trying to attain, with unbending logic, the goal that she had set herself. Her objective was dual: to feminise and to enslave. The transformation would allow crucial progress: the opportunity to exploit it had arisen to make Fred come one step closer to enslavement. Léontine had seized this opportunity and was exploiting it to the full, no more, no less. Her ideas of sophistication and procrastination had no other motives.

That is why, on the following day, she broached the subject of earrings again:

"Frédérique, you are probably very conscious of my determination to make you wear those pendants which I bought you. When my mind is set on something, I always get my way. But it won't be done by a jeweller, for I do not want to witness another scene; we shall remain at home and I shall execute the deed myself."

Fred looked at his aunt but did not answer. She paused and continued,

"I wanted to warn you because I want to give you time to see reason. You see, Frédérique, in life, you have to resign yourself to the inevitable. The only thing that matters here is my will and when I command, remonstrations are a waste of time. I expect total obedience from you; this incident is well-timed to test your meekness and reveal your willingness. And, you know that if you resist, if you rebel, it won't make one jot of difference. I said a week; in exactly one week, on the hour, it shall be done whether you like it or not."

She paused again to maximise the effect of her words and continued, in an unctuous tone,

"A final word of advice, for I do not wish to give you an unpleasant shock. It is far more painful than you have been told. Yesterday, the sales assistant misled you by assuring you that you would feel nothing. He wanted to reassure you so as to overcome your preposterously intractable resistance. In reality, it is brief but extremely painful. Surely you are not gullible enough to believe that a needle, even one made of gold, can penetrate a substantial thickness of flesh without being noticeable? The pain is intense but also very brief. You have hardly had time to suffer before it is over. All things considered, it is an unpleasant but bearable moment; we have all been through it, have we not? When the time comes, you will be brave and afterwards, you will forget all about it."

These words created the desired effect: Fred came to feel an ineffable repulsion for this ear-piercing and a strong desire to avoid it; for a week, he could think of nothing else.

One day, he happened across a page from Augustin Thierry's *Tales of Merovingian Times* (which Madame de Saint-Genest had probably left open deliberately) describing the incisions which the Merovingians performed on the ears of their slaves so as to recognise them easily if they escaped. Fred established a parallel and came to the conclusion that an incision on a male ear was shameful and degrading, and he saw the piercing of the lobe as an updated version of that Merovingian custom. He even read the story of young Prince Leudaste who, at a similar age, had to endure the same life-long mark which stayed with him even when he rose to power and honours. Fred identified with Leudaste.

One of the plates in the book depicted the child tied to a post by his wrists and ankles and held by one man while another pierced his ears. The child was struggling and looked terrified: the scene was clearly an ordeal. Fred immediately believed that, in addition to being degrading, the promised perforation would be a form of torture, and the vision of this crying, screaming and struggling child against that post became an omen of what lay in store and stayed with him to intensify his apprehension.

As for the Baroness, she exploited every possible opportunity to keep him in this state of dreadful anticipation.

One evening at dinner, she took a cork from a bottle and said to Rose:

"I will need a cork larger than this one and it must be immaculate of course; you place it behind the ear and it receives the needle after it has been pushed through the flesh."

Fred heard every word and his fears redoubled. He was distraught and expected the worst.

At last, the fateful day was upon him. Fred awoke earlier than usual and pricked up his ears at the slightest sound, but nothing was different and he remained nonplussed, not daring to ask any questions. The truth was that Madame de Saint-Genest had decreed that the ceremony should take place in the evening; she wanted Fred to spend the day in the throes of anguish. Moreover, the *mise-en-scène* which she had devised included specific lighting effects.

At various moments of the day, she sent someone out to buy accessories such as bandages, cotton-wool or antiseptic; she made sure that these orders were given out within Fred's earshot and on each occasion, she would specify to Rose that the object in question was to play a part in the minor operation.

Soon, dusk began to soften contours.

Fred was in his room, dressed in girls' clothes, as on any other day now that there were no other clothes in his wardrobe. He was seated, gnawed by fear.

Suddenly, he started. Someone opened the door: it was Rose.

She ambled towards him, concealing something shiny behind her back before furtively laying it on a table.

"Mademoiselle Frédérique," she said, "Madame awaits you in her boudoir."

This sentence brought his fear to a climax and

his heart started pounding. Rose took advantage of his agitation to swiftly move behind him and seize his wrists which she joined behind his back. Fred thrashed about but Rose's clenched hands were like a vice. She managed to check his disorderly movements and led him backwards to the table where she had discreetly and deftly placed a pair of handcuffs.

Without too much trouble, she succeeded in putting them around his wrists which were soon trapped in two rings joined by a short chain of only two or three links. Madame de Saint-Genest had hunted them down herself and had had some difficulty in finding them for she needed rings that were small enough to prevent a thirteen year-old boy's hands from slipping out.

Startled by the cold contact of the steel and the click of the spring, Fred found himself a prisoner before he knew it.

When he saw that his hands were chained behind his back and that he could no longer move his arms, he protested.

"Those are Madame's orders." explained Rose. "If you weren't so stubborn, we wouldn't have to resort to such stratagems."

"I refuse to be chained up!"

"Too late! Complain as you may, rope would have cut into your flesh, whereas with these cuffs, your wrists won't get bruised, even if the operation takes longer than anticipated."

"Will it take long?" enquired Fred in a voice strained by anxiety.

"One never can tell with you...It all depends

Surpris par le froid de l'acier et le claquement des ressorts....

on your behaviour. Let's not dawdle: Madame might become impatient."

On saying this, she led him to the door and pushed him into the corridor. Fred could not resist properly; besides, it was not his intention. He had been highly-strung since awaking and he was now experiencing an anti-climax. All that remained in his mind was an overwhelming fear of this terrible unknown fate which awaited him.

Chapter Seven

The Ear-piercing

Having reached the door of the boudoir, Rose knocked hard twice.

"Come in!" said Léontine in a lilting voice.

Fred thought that the door would open onto Hades and nearly cried out in astonishment when, on the contrary, he discovered a heavenly vision, a scene out of a fairytale.

The boudoir, with which he was not well acquainted, having been allowed in only a few times, had been specially prepared for the occasion. Pastel-coloured chiffon hung hither and thither like scarves made of clouds; brightly-coloured silk cushions embroidered with gold were scattered artistically and untidily; a myriad of flowers blossomed everywhere, in crystal or *flambé* stoneware vases, in delicate and fragile Venetian glassware, exquisite works of art which reflected or refracted the light. But above all, these riches and ornaments were softly bathed in a magical blue light. The ceiling light had been switched off and this fantastical lighting was given out by blue lightbulbs dotted around the room, one beneath a lampshade of superimposed petals, another inside a translucent vase, a third amid a light spray of greenery.

Entranced by the magical charm of this decor, Fred at first had not noticed his aunt; when he saw her, he forgot these heavenly surroundings and transferred all his awe onto this goddess. Her prodigious figure was in a corner decked with flowers and suffused with that soft mysterious light which gave an almost tactile quality to the perfume which hung in the air.

At that moment, he saw only her back. She was standing before a mirror and was patting her hair into shape with her fingers which glittered with rings. Her full, elegant figure was revealed by the translucent folds of a gossamer *negligé* trimmed with lace; her arms were naked — the sleeves being so short that they barely existed at all. As she lifted them gracefully, their harmonious rounded contours could be seen and in that light, their milky whiteness became transparent like alabaster. Her full bosom, her slender waist, her rounded hips and admirably-shaped legs, in conjunction with the light-coloured *negligé*, amounted to the most perfect and voluptuously enticing figure.

Fred could admire her at leisure for she continued to be absorbed by vanity. When she finally turned round, she offered, in these surroundings, in this light, in this casual dress, such luminous and spellbinding beauty as to become imprinted on Fred's memory forever. On two or three occasions, she had appeared to him in finery or in poses which had hinted at her magnificent physical beauty; but this time, she was so ravishing and alluring that she erased all his previous visions.

Fred, en découvrant cette prestigieuse silhouette... (Chap. VII).

That had precisely been Léontine's intention and she read her achievement in the child's wide, unblinking and enraptured eyes.

Rose and Fred stood a few feet from the door, the maid's hand rested on the youth's shoulder while the other held the chain of the handcuffs.

Léontine walked up to them, her majestic feet gliding over the thick carpet, she circled them, considered the chained wrists, tested the sturdiness of the fetters and coolly sat on a couch strewn with cushions.

"So you have brought me our young and unruly prisoner," she said to Rose. "She resembles a princess captured by pirates and sold on some slave market where you have just purchased her for me."

"A similar thought had occurred to me," answered the maid, on seeing Madame looking as beautiful as a Sultana out of *The Arabian Nights*.

This amused Léontine who let out a tinkling laugh. She went on:

"You skilful supplier, come nearer; I have a few orders to give you which do not concern the other slave."

Rose rejoined in her laughter and, under the domineering spell of the Baroness, kept up the game by lifting a hand to her forehead and advancing in a deferential and bowed manner. She then knelt in front of the couch and waited. Madame de Saint-Genest leaned over to whisper a series of recommendations; she concluded, out loud, with the words, "Do you understand? Now, go!"

Before rising to her feet, Rose kowtowed and

solemnly kissed the diffident Baroness' feet.

Fred did not miss a thing; it was the continuation of the dream which had begun when the door had been opened. He came to a rather abrupt awakening when Rose grabbed him again and led him to a large Renaissance easy-chair which had been placed in the middle of the room, right under the ceiling light.

Fred was pushed into the chair and instinctively gave a start like a convict on the rack. His rapture melted, his resignation faded and he instantly resumed his unruly and enraged ways which had been so resistant to discipline. He tried to stand up but Rose stopped him; he began to kick out erratically and knocked over the maid who had stooped to pick up a bundle of rope from under the easy-chair.

Léontine rose to her feet and came to the maid's assistance. She stood behind the chair and pinioned Fred, who was thrashing about in an alarming fashion, while Rose hurriedly tied the child's ankles to the chair legs. After this precautionary measure, all that was needed was to wind some rope around his torso and the back of the chair so that Fred was completely immobilised.

Unable to move, he started to scream.

"Be quiet!" snapped Léontine. "You refuse to be silent? You want to scream some more? Rose, stuff this handkerchief into his mouth as a gag."

She handed Rose a handkerchief rolled up in a ball; the maid, at the risk of getting bitten,

Fred regardait de tous ses yeux (Chap. VII).

pushed it into his mouth.

At first, Fred experienced a strange sensation for he could smell, with intoxicating intensity, the perfume on his aunt's handkerchief and this temporarily obliterated his discomfort; but soon, the more unpleasant sensations prevailed and, his mouth filling with saliva and feeling on the brink of suffocation, he looked imploringly at his aunt.

"Very well! I'll remove your gag but you must promise to be quiet. One scream during the operation is acceptable. But it is totally unnecessary at this juncture."

Rose removed the gag and brought up a pedestal table to lay out the indispensable accessories.

Remaining true to her new tactic, Léontine stopped her:

"One moment! Frédérique is so nervous that I think it best that she should not see all these preparations. Blindfold her."

Rose obeyed, seized a silk scarf and duly placed it over Fred's eyes, though a little too high so that he could still witness the proceedings.

Still smirking, Rose approached the pedestal table covered not only in the utensils for the operation, but also some totally irrelevant objects whose sole purpose was to look foreboding so as to heighten the build-up.

Fred's mind was not exactly at ease and beads of perspiration stood out on his temples. Rose was going about her preparations in a leisurely and methodical manner. She rubbed surgical spirit onto a cork and lit a small stove to sterilize the needle.

"Now all is set," said Léontine. "Rose, remove the blindfold; it is best if my niece sees the proceedings. Pain can be aggravated by the unknown."

This constituted another element of Madame de Saint-Genest's plan: she wanted to be clearly seen by the patient; she was anxious that he should see as much as feel. Piercing his ears was not enough: they had to be pierced by his aunt in person, by a woman who had wanted to surpass her own beauty and had succeeded. She wanted Fred to be perfectly aware of the identity of the hand who was hurting and marking him. She wanted her radiant and statuesque beauty to be associated with violence, pain and blood.

"The time has come," announced Léontine. "Frédérique, I beseech you, be quiet or else I will be annoyed and my movements need to be precise if I am to spare you pain."

Fred heard a few clicks and there was a change of scene.

The Baroness pressed a few light switches and turned out all the blue lights. Then the ceiling light came on and Fred's face was brightly flooded.

The blue dreamlike glow had vanished and in the brightness which made necklaces, bracelets and rings twinkle, Fred could make out the ripe beauty of this pretty blond and half-naked tormentor who brandished a long gold needle.

"Are you ready, Rose?" she asked.

The chambermaid stepped behind the easy-chair, grabbed Fred's head with both hands and pinned one cheek to the back of the chair. A few feet away, Madame de Saint-Genest was sterilizing the gold needle.

Fred was beside himself with terror; he expected a smarting pain and prayed that it would soon be over.

Léontine touched his ear, slowly as if to caress him, slipped the cork behind his pink and delicate lobe; then, just as Fred's tension had reached its climax, she said, "Rose, you have forgotten the disinfectant. But don't move: I see you are busy. I'll get it."

She moved away but it was a decoy to carefully and noiselessly switch off the ceiling light.

"That's all we needed! A power cut!" exclaimed the Baroness. "We could have done without this setback."

"Should I switch on the lamps?"

"No, Rose. I wouldn't be able to see properly; I need all the light I can get, let us wait until the power is restored."

This unexpected incident had deeply perturbed Fred. By being deferred yet again, his ordeal seemed unbearable. The room had suddenly been plunged into almost total darkness: only the stove was on and emitted a flickering flame, blue and green like on the surface of punch, which only lit those objects adjacent to it.

A fantastical glow leapt up whimsically; bizarre reflections spangled the room, shimmering lights flew up and then died. In this vacillating glow which made the shadows darker still, Léontine's silhouette had altered once again. It had become imprecise and alarming; the only light on her body was the flashing of her gold bracelets and her rings, and the animated gleam of her eyes and teeth.

When the Baroness deemed that the interval had lasted long enough to put Fred's nerves to the test, she restored the light, flooded the torture chair as well as every nook and cranny and became her former self, namely a radiant blond beauty highlighted by her glittering jewellery.

Rose grabbed Fred's head again and positioned his ear correctly. Madame de Saint-Genest approached, holding the gold needle in one hand and the cork in the other.

She was about to perform the operation when she was seized by a violent emotion: she was not afraid of being clumsy, after all, she intended to make her nephew suffer more than necessary; no, she was simply conscious of being on the verge of fulfilling her dearest wish, one which had first occurred to her when she had collected Fred from Sainte-Brigitte where ear-piercing had been mentioned during a conversation with Mrs. Stockley. It was also a dream which she had cherished lovingly for an entire week of communion and elation, a dream which was about to become realised, which was to be the magnificent culmination of all her endeavours...

Eager to savour this moment, she prolonged it. She moved in front of Fred so that he could clearly see the instrument of torture and could behold the prestigious figure of his delightful

Rose, retirez le bandeau, maintenant (Chap. VII).

tormentor.

Indeed, Fred devoured her with his eyes, then stared at the gold needle and shuddered. His gaze reverted to her naked arms, her ostentatious *décolletage* and her prominent bust and his terror subsided a little.

Léontine had not been mistaken in her calculations; intimidated by this ceremonial, unnerved by the long wait, Fred was in such a state that the piercing would carry profound repercussions in his entire being and, thanks to its awe-inspiring detail, would be akin to an unforgettable rite of passage. His flesh, his brain, his nerves, his very character, both superficially and intimately, would be affected by this incision.

Although Fred was angry and frightened, he no longer felt refractory as he would have done if it had been performed by his teachers at Sainte-Brigitte. He would have struggled violently, he would have shrieked, frothed at the mouth and bitten them; he would have warned them and would have carried out his threat. But because his executioner was his beautiful aunt, the ordeal seemed less repulsive and shameful; furthermore, — a strange phenomenon which proved how much Léontine possessed him — all other feelings were overshadowed by the fear of pain and the dread of blood-letting.

Having made sure that the cork was in place, the Baroness pulled back her hand holding the gold needle. At that moment, she understood the dispositions of those matrons in ancient Rome who derived pleasure from piercing their black or white slaves with a sharp instrument attached to a gold ring which they would slip onto their finger. More to the point, she could empathise with them and, casting a glance at the looking-glass, she realised that she had also adopted their appearance. This young prisoner in chains, immobilised by his bonds, and this pretty, submissive maid who pandered to her every whim and, a few moments ago, had prostrated herself at her feet, were they not her slaves?

Calm, determined and feeling like a goddess who possesses the power of life and death, she stabbed this enslaved flesh which was her nephew's ear.

Fred screamed and Léontine's cool vanished. Her blood ran cold and her heart lurched sharply in response to Fred's yell.

The tip of the needle had not completely penetrated the ear. Madame de Saint-Genest did not pull the needle out but, with a sharp jolt, pushed it into the cork. When she removed the needle, a drop of blood appeared and swelled: Fred's first drop earring was a ruby which glittered beneath the ceiling light.

But Léontine was not finished yet. She thrust a thicker needle into the tiny aperture: she wanted to enlarge the hole so as to ensure that it would never close up; she also wanted to eke out the pain, she did not want him to get off so lightly. She succeeded in wringing a few moans and screams out of him.

With the help of Rose, she cleaned and dabbed

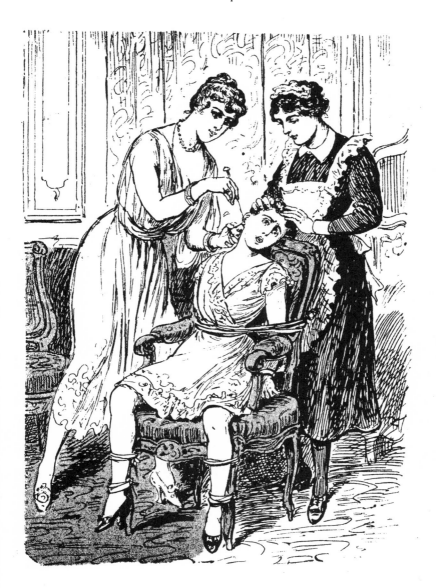

Elle comprenait la mentalité des matrones romaines (Ch. VI)

the wound, and made sure that Fred saw his own blood on the dressings; she then proceeded with the cauterization which made him grind his teeth.

She repeated the ritual on the other ear, aggravated the preliminaries, dragged them out, made two attempts and finally mangled the wound. Fred went through the same pangs and let out the same screams.

At last, the irreversible deed was over. Fred's ears were smarting, evidence of an open wound which would scar but would never disappear.

Never before had he undergone such a profound transformation: his ears were now those of a girl.

Rose made him swallow a cordial and untied his torso and legs. Meanwhile, Madame de Saint-Genest switched off the ceiling light, restored the blue glow and returned to her seat on the embroidered cushions.

Lolling on her elbows in a pose which befitted her domineering indolence, her gaze followed her young prisoner's every move. She noticed that this infinitesimal detail, namely these two tiny holes in his lobes already altered his face: it was conspicuous, eye-catching. Even without wearing earrings, he would look feminine; she suddenly realised the consequences of this ear-piercing and thrilled with pleasure: he would never again be able to wear male clothing without being noticed. It was tantamount to asserting that, from now on, he was condemned to feminine dress.

Rose's voice roused her from her daydream.

The maid asked her, "Shall I remove the handcuffs?"

"Not just yet; not before he has begged forgiveness for his fractious behaviour and his yells."

The maid pushed the child towards his aunt. With his hands behind his back, Fred approached the haughty woman bathed in a magical glow and heady fragrances. She looked at him with a condescending smile, but her regal grace was mitigated by an affectionate tenderness. Fred was subjugated, dazzled by the radiance of her jewellery and her naked skin, so white and diaphanous, he was intoxicated by the rare fragrances and the delicate smell of her blond hair and her body which was virtually naked under the lawn and the lace.

He sunk to his knees and, like Rose before him, prostrated himself, but longer and more meekly; he devotedly kissed her small, authoritative, arched foot shod in high-heeled evening shoes and covered with an openwork silk stocking which clung tenuously and shimmeringly to the pink transparency of her ankle and leg.

Grovelling and subjected like never before, he falteringly begged for forgiveness and she placed her other foot on his head and knew that he belonged to her completely and forever now that she had drawn his blood and branded her indelible mark in his flesh.

Whereas she was proud of having marked an animate being, Fred was ashamed of having been branded. This dyad of feelings can be observed especially when two beings are in conflict and one

Elle sentit qu'il lui appartenait bien pour toujours (Chap. VII)

succeeds in dominating and taming the other.[4] It heralded with certainty that in the future, if the Baroness willed it, a master/slave relationship would be established between the aunt and her nephew.

It so happened that she willed it with all her heart.

---

[4] This observation can also be found in the studies which compose the series *Les Asservies* (*The Enslaved*) by Don Brennus Aléra, illustrated by Tack and published by Select-Bibliothèque.

Chapter Eight

The First Pair of Earrings

In the wake of this episode, Fred would often relive in his dreams the horrors of his painful initiation which had marked the dawn of a new life.

Even his mind was changing in the aftermath of the shock. In the past, he had been able to remember that he was a boy temporarily in feminine attire. But now this thought never occurred to him. He was convinced that he had undergone a sex change. There was no doubt, in his still innocent mind, that he could never revert to his former gender now that a painful and bloody operation had permanently transformed him into a girl.

This firm belief made Madame de Saint-Genest's task easier: Fred accepted to wear the frocks and bodices, high-heeled shoes and constricting corsets which were his lot; he accepted to devote his time to needlework and tapestry and, above all, he no longer baulked at answering to the name of 'Frédérique' which before had made him wince.

The wound on his ear took a month to heal completely and during most of that time, Léontine took advantage of his recent shock to inculcate in him all those little details which set girls apart. She knew that one day, under the influence of daily routine, even his tastes would become feminine.

As soon as she noticed that the lobes were healed, prompted by her taste for pomp and her instinct for drama, she organised a sort of unveiling ceremony for she knew that it would have an effect on the youth.

"Frédérique," she said, "come and see me in my boudoir at two o'clock. Be dressed and ready to go out and we shall go for a drive."

When Fred entered the boudoir, where he had not set foot since the ear-piercing episode, he was brutally assailed by a rush of memories: he visualised the room in the way it was at the time with its plethora of flowers, its riot of scents and its lighting effects. His aunt, however, seemed as beautiful to him now as she did then.

Yet, she was now dressed differently in a close-fitting town outfit which emphasised her full figure; her arms were concealed beneath *glacé* kid gloves which reached up to her shoulders, whereas her stockinged round legs were visible between a short skirt and tall boots, dizzyingly high and extravagantly arched, and her cleavage was revealed, framed by a shameless *décolletage*.

She was the same Léontine, but sterner and more statuesque in this outdoor attire which only lacked a hat. The emotions which stirred within him were not lost on Léontine; she did not rein them in, for if recent events came flooding back, they would never be forgotten.

At last she said;

"Now that your ears are healed, you are going to wear your first pair of earrings."

She made him sit next to her and fastened a pair of pendants to his small ears. Her gentle gloved hands, the same which, not so long ago, had hurt him so much, now brushed against his ears like a sincere caress. Fred remained contentedly passive. She then exclaimed her admiration at the way in which this pair of rings — commonly called creoles — embellished his features and she led him to a looking-glass so that he could see for himself. Fred had to concede that he looked prettier and thought, though without voicing it, that they even conferred a quirky charm to his face.

"Keep them on," ordered Léontine, "you will always wear a pair, these or others; I shall tell you when to change them."

Satisfied by the sight of his lively and impish face looking more effeminate, Léontine was eager to show off her nephew — or more exactly 'her niece' as she liked to say and think of him — to society. She placed a hat on her frothy mass of hair and secured it with a fairly long pin with a large pearl at one end. The blushing Fred recognised the gold needle which had been used to pierce his ears.

"Well spotted, it is the same pin which drew a few drops of blood from your ears." said Léontine.

During the ride, Léontine was satisfied to note that not a single passer-by sensed something amiss. On the contrary, among the compliments which were addressed to her, she overheard the words, "what a pretty young lady!" on several occasions.

As for Frédérique, he could not avert his eyes from her hat skewered with this gold pin tipped with a baroque pearl.

That evening at dinner, he was seated facing his aunt and was astonished to see the pin on her boudoir dress: it now served as a brooch to narrow the slit of her *décolletage* between her pink marmoreal breasts. He could consequently no longer look at his aunt without being forever reminded of the scene which had left him terrified, hurt, bleeding, humiliated, feminised and branded.

During the following weeks, Léontine played with her nephew as if he were a doll. She made him wear, for a few days at a time, a succession of earrings which she had purchased specially for him. She tried them all on, took pleasure in the changes she made to his face, but preferred the larger pairs which, on account of their weight, kept the holes intact and ensured that they would never close up, even if, for one reason or another, Frédérique temporarily gave up wearing earrings.

On more than one occasion, she made him wear long and weighty jet pendants which looked bizarre against his jaw, increased the whiteness of his skin and framed his pure oval face in an unexpected manner.

One day, whilst tidying the few knick-knacks lying at the bottom of Fred's trunk, Léontine came across some strange contraptions adorned with bells and questioned him about them. He explained that

Cette invention amusa beaucoup la baronne (Chap. VIII).

he had had to wear them around his wrists and neck at Sainte-Brigitte to punish him for trying to escape. Mrs. Stockley's invention greatly amused the Baroness and she insisted on seeing her nephew decked out in this way. When he had donned the bells, she added some to his ears: two little bells attached to rings were made into pendants which tinkled every time he moved his head.

When she deemed Fred well-acquainted with his new, eminently feminine jewels, she carried out an experiment. On a day when she was entertaining two lady friends, she rang for her chambermaid and ordered her to send Mademoiselle Frédérique to the drawing-room. Out of caution, she had made a point of choosing dusk, being wary of feminine shrewdness. She introduced 'her niece' to the two ladies and dismissed her before asking for the lights to be switched on. Everything went smoothly; Fred introduced herself like a well-bred, reserved and polite young lady, gracefully took her leave and withdrew without a hitch. Judging from their comments, neither guest had detected the slightest hint of boyishness. Absolutely not. They merely complimented their beautiful friend by saying that her niece showed promise of rivalling her aunt in beauty, though in a different way; and nothing more was said.

This test convinced Madame de Saint-Genest: in a month, she would wipe the slate clean. Rose, who was shortly to wed, would be provided with a dowry and was moving to a far-flung region of France: the Pyrenees. On the pretext of a long journey, the other servants were dismissed and not replaced. Léontine did indeed feign a departure but returned a few days later and hired new staff who were merely told that they were entering the service of the Baroness Saint-Genest who lived alone with her niece, Mademoiselle de Montignac, said to be a pretty orphan.

Chapter Nine

A Page in Petticoats

At present, nobody in the mansion of the rue de Varenne, aside from Léontine de Saint-Genest, knew the real sex of Mademoiselle Frédérique. Nobody suspected that his ears had been pierced only a few months ago, forcibly and with such bizarre ritual.

Steeped in this new environment, young de Montignac gradually forgot his real gender and felt comfortable with the role which he was forced to play. This was partly due to his living conditions but it was mainly his passionate admiration for his aunt which prompted his acceptance and his continual wearing of earrings remained of crucial importance.

Fred had been right to fear those earrings, for they unquestionably possess an uncanny power to feminise; dress, bearing and gestures are inevitably brought into harmony with that characteristic ornament. As for the rest, women's clothes, corsets, suspenders, shoes and the most effeminate jewels, they can be worn like any other clothes. Unisex items of clothing can admittedly vary in cut, colour and aspect. But, when all is said and done, these differences are merely superficial and once these accessories have been removed, there is no way of telling that they were ever worn. Earrings, however, are quite another matter: to be able to wear them, one must have pierced ears and for Fred, this initiation had been particularly traumatic: he looked in the mirror all too often not to notice the blatantly visible stigma. When he removed his drop earrings before retiring to bed, he felt as if he was bearing an indelible mark which immediately caught the eye. Like it or not, he had to continue wearing female clothes if he did not want to be noticed. He no longer had any choice in the matter, female dress had become indispensable to him: furthermore, if he did not want to attract attention, he also had to wear these clothes with the utmost ease, elegance and grace.

So Frédérique reasoned herself into becoming coquettish. After a while, she would be coquettish out of habit and finally one day, she would be motivated by inclination only.

Of course, the Baroness' niece had not yet reached that stage. If she was to be initiated to all the trappings of feminine elegance, she certainly needed long hair. Madame de Saint-Genest knew that it would take two to two and a half years. Only then would her hair be long enough to style into a bun. Léontine was aware that she had to be patient, and she had as much patience as willpower and was determined to let nothing get in the way of the achievement of her enterprise. She would be all the more patient given that Frédérique was still very young; in two or three years time, she would be of age to come out in society.

There was time enough to prepare the accomplished young girl who, a few years from now, would make her mark on Parisian *salons.*

In the same way as she had suited clothes and finery to the girl's age, the Baroness now applied the same method to books. Frédérique's bookcase was exclusively stocked with books written for girls of her age and these carefully selected tomes perfected the slow and daily business of wearing skirts, bodices and other feminine paraphernalia. Even if the saying goes, "it is not the cowl that makes the monk," clothes are more often than not taken at face value and pervade not only one's behaviour, demeanour, gait and gestures, but also one's thoughts and even one's opinions. A person will think or behave differently depending on whether he or she is wearing trousers or a skirt.

For Léontine, this theory was amply borne out by the physical and psychological development of 'her niece'.

It has to be said that Léontine had no difficulty in keeping Frédérique within the confines of the occupations, studies and even entertainment befitting girls of her age. Frédérique's bursts of resistance were less frequent, she would content herself with an upsurge of ill-humour or a sour face. Madame de Saint-Genest had predicted this profound change in Fred's fiery temper, or else she would never have let Rose leave her service. Had there been the slightest glimmer of her having to tussle with a furious little scoundrel, she would have kept this invaluable assistant, so resourceful and docile and who had understood her so well as to anticipate her every wish.

She had sensed that Fred's education was entering a new phase, she had assessed the extent of her power over him. To bend him to her whims, which all focused on the same goal, she relied more on her prestige than on anything else and she was right in doing so. At most, only a few slaps or a spanking were necessary.

The Baroness had not replaced Rose, at least, not with someone to wait upon her personally. She had hired a new chambermaid whose duties were restricted to cleaning, washing and sewing. She answered the door, ran errands and only once daily did she enter Léontine's suite, namely in the morning to attend to her ablutions and to style her hair, for these tasks were still a little too arduous for young Frédérique.

But Frédérique was now in charge of all the other personal duties. Satisfying her penchant for a delicate and refined service, the beautiful widow had gradually taught Frédérique all the duties which are incumbent upon a well-trained chambermaid. He took his duties so seriously that he would get up before her to bring her cocoa in bed. He dressed, shod and gloved her, brushed down and put away her frocks, took care of her shoes and jewels and became acquainted with the innumerable accessories that are to be found in an elegant dressing-room: its various utensils, bottles, creams, powders, all those things which enhance beauty, preserve it and finally supplant it when it declines.

Ce fut ainsi que, trois jours par semaine... (Chap. IX).

The Baroness had become akin to the lady of the manor waited upon by a page; but that page's dexterity, skill and nimbleness were like his dress: they were a girl's.

Once Fred had grown a little, it suddenly occurred to Léontine that he could be trained to wait at table. It would no longer be a *tête-à-tête* between them in the privacy of her suite given that her domestic staff would witness the service performed by Mademoiselle de Montignac. So, one day, she explained that a young lady could never become an accomplished hostess if she did not have a little knowledge in every department and consequently, Mademoiselle de Montignac would alternate with the maid to wait at table.

Three days a week, with a napkin over his arm, a bibbed apron over his dress and wearing his earrings, Fred would correctly present dishes to his beautiful aunt and wait until she had finished her coffee before dining in his turn.

To obtain this result, Madame de Saint-Genest resorted to cuffs on the ear or spankings, but never more than necessary. She preferred to clearly voice her orders, frown with authority or gesture commandingly with her beautiful naked or gloved arms; she would also make the most of the fascination she exerted over the child by pinning *that* gold needle to her bodice to conjure up the blue-lit boudoir where a blond Sultana sat, enthroned, an exquisite tormentor and an irresistible dominatrice.

Chapter Ten

A Revelation

In the space of a few weeks, Fred became a very skilled and resourceful maid. Feminine dress had a real influence over his nature: his gestures became calmer and steadier and all his actions were imbued with totally feminine deftness and expertise. He was growing up of course, and this rendered him more capable of carrying out these household chores.

He was indeed growing up...

This came to Léontine's attention, as she watched him in silence, mulling over some obscure musings, peculiar desires or incoherent longings which she probably could not define herself. At that moment, her bold and determined eyes lit up with a strange and perverse gleam which betokened an ardent sensuality and made one wonder why she had remained such a discreet widow for seven years.

He was growing up, but clothed in this feminine dress, he was so profoundly changed that a stranger would have found it very difficult to tell his exact age.

Léontine could not ignore the fact that he would soon turn fourteen and that he was not quite a child any more. One day, her meek and nimble chambermaid would turn into an Adonis in feminine clothes.

Certain clues pointed to his impending adolescence. Fred no longer looked at his aunt in the same way. He had admittedly always responded to her harmonious and stately figure, to her firm and elegantly full curves, the enticing milkiness of her plump and firm flesh glimpsed in the plunging neckline of her bodice or in the broadening of her hips, the precise and perfect shape of her domineeringly arched foot in its kid casket, or the compelling shape of her statuesque arm, provocatively naked or tightly sheathed in *glacé* leather.

For a long time, his eyes had reflected nothing more than instinctive admiration and speechless satisfaction. Now, however, his gaze had become mature and probing, it singled out certain details, it welcomed her beauty revealed time and time again by certain graceful poses, various refinements of finery or clothing, artful devices of coquettishness or certain lighting effects which flattered the curves of her limbs or the hues of her flesh.

Surely this could not be exclusively put down to the artistic admiration instilled in him by a spinster fond of music and watercolour painting, who came to teach him accomplishments. There was more to it than that: it was obvious from the fleeting and sporadic gleams in his eyes, which had become more frequent of late. Above all, he *wanted* to see: in the morning, when he brought in her breakfast on a tray, when her nightgown hung only by one satin strap making her breasts peek through the lace; or when the chambermaid, before styling

Léontine's fine, blond hair, bared her sloping shoulders, the marked curve of her nape and the velvety furrow of her plump back. When they went out, her flesh was hidden beneath silk or velvet, kid or fur and offered a fragmented vision which was far more attractive because it had to be sought out. All day, around the house, when she moved her gracefully curved arms or lifted them above her head, she would divulge the secret recess of her armpits. When she nonchalantly crossed her legs, she revealed her calves. When she leaned forward, her cleavage was put on show and drew the gaze like a magnet.

Léontine intended to train Fred to wait on her even more intimately. She wanted him to replace her chambermaid as soon as he had learnt how to style hair. But it was crucial that he should learn this routine early on so that when he grew older, he would continue to serve her unthinkingly, like an automaton.

There was one drawback in delaying his training. So, taking advantage of the chambermaid's three-day absence, Madame de Saint-Genest decided that it would be 'her niece's' duty to help her out of her bath.

The following morning, Léontine rang and the youth entered the bathroom. He was a little abashed on entering, but soon regained his composure when he saw that only her head emerged from the suds. Following his aunt's orders, he opened the airing-cupboard and had her bathrobe and towels at the ready.

But when the Baroness stepped out of the water, it was quite another matter. Fred was fairly taken aback by this first and sudden revelation of female nudity. He felt an indescribable concatenation of surprise, admiration and curiosity which left him open-mouthed, wide-eyed and rooted to the spot. A heathen witnessing the birth of Venus would have been prey to the same inner turmoil. To him, his aunt, streaming with pearl-like droplets, was Venus incarnate.

Never in his wildest dreams had he imagined that a body could be as perfect or as dazzling in its paleness and marmoreal firmness. In truth, he had imagined nothing, having no knowledge of naked women.

Dazzled by this splendour, it never occurred to him that other women could equally own similar wonders beneath their frocks. He was under the irrational belief that no woman could bear a remote resemblance to his aunt and consequently considered Léontine exceptional, blessed with unique gifts and created after a flawless prototype to rule with her beauty over the human race in general and himself in particular.

Her charms assailed his concentration and he did not have time to come to his senses, to marvel at his recent discovery of her plump waist, rounded hips, belly polished like an ivory shield and fleshy thighs before Léontine, her back turned to him, exclaimed a little testily,

"Come along, Frédérique, my robe!"

He wrapped her in the warm cotton which

Ebloui par cette splendeur radieuse, Fred... (Chap. **X**).

clung to her full bosom, her jutting hips, her heavenly legs and generous rump whose full, firm spheres he could feel against his body.

Once his gaze had explored her ravishing thirty-year old body in all its radiance and appetising glory, his hands dried her limbs and similarly explored her curves emphasised by the wet linen, like the wet cloth with which sculptors shroud a fresh lump of clay which yields forth the statue of a goddess.

When he stooped to dry her round, dimpled knees and long, firm calves, he embraced them and succumbed to his adoration by dropping to his knees, prostrating himself and showering with kisses her pink toes with their gem-like toenails. So spontaneous and so impulsive was his reaction that it had caused her robe to fall, evoking the image of the white greyhound curled at her feet like Mademoiselle de Maupin's *chemise*. The Baroness stood naked in the middle of the room whose white earthenware tiles reflected the light and illuminated her flesh.

She was standing in front of a mirror and could see herself, motionless and regal, dominating with her imposing presence the annihilated child who seemed crushed by an invisible hand at the feet of a magnificent statue of flesh.

Léontine wavered for a moment with regards to her line of conduct: should she dismiss her niece and dress alone?

She did not hesitate for long and soon arrived at a conclusion:

If I want Frédérique to become an agreeable and useful slave, he must get used to seeing me naked...We are out of the wood now and it is the perfect opportunity to get him to see my body and to caress my skin. So let's press on!

Having made this decision, she consented to everything that would lead to the fulfilment of her fantasy and placed herself in Frédérique's hands as if nothing had happened.

She could have curtailed the incident by asking for a kimono and oriental mules to be brought to her and retiring to her room. But he might have inferred that she was frightened of him when, on the contrary, it was he who had to be frightened of her beauty. She was anxious that no detail should be omitted from the usual ritual. She remained naked and showed Fred how to pour perfumes onto her body and how to rub her down with the massage glove. She wanted to make him understand that he did not matter.

Fred performed his duties with devoted adoration, as if he were worshipping a beautiful apparition from another dimension, a divine being who could vanish at any moment.

This beginning in the white bathroom was the counterpart to the blue-lit boudoir in Fred's existence and memory. The revelation of female nudity was pivotal in itself, not to mention being asked to feel this appetising flesh and to caress these wondrous curves, and not just with his eyes! As a result, his mouth was dry, his temples pounded and his eyes sparkled. Léontine congratulated herself for having trained him before the child gave way to the young man.

Fred behaved as in an intoxicated daydream. He was only just conscious enough to hear Léontine's orders as she pointed to various bottles and explained their use.

She spared him nothing, neither the delicate lingerie, nor the *negligé*, nor the slippers; he was compelled to assist her right to the end as if he were a girl accustomed to playing this role every day.

Finally, they went their separate ways to attend to their usual duties: Fred spent the morning tidying, dusting and changing the flowers in the vases, all this feverishly, as if to numb his senses.

He only saw his aunt again at luncheon, which he served correctly and in silence, barely daring to look at her.

The bath episode had increased Madame de Saint-Genest's hold over him, a hold that was already strong; as for Fred, he was edging ever closer to enslavement.

The Baroness, who had been watching him on the sly during the entire meal, mused, as he was bringing in the coffee,

"I'll make a girl out of him and that's settled. There's nothing in this world that can prevent the miracle from happening."

Chapter Eleven

Beneath the Heel of Venus

Having lunched on his own, Fred went up to his room; he had an hour to spare before his piano lesson. He stopped in front of the mirror, as was often the case, for he liked to see the effect of the earrings he was wearing that day now that he had become more comfortable with his physical metamorphosis.

During this contemplation, he occasionally touched up a fold or puffed out a ribbon; sometimes he would go so far as to hold his skirt between index and thumb to curtsey, or hitch it up to look at his shoes, or twirl coquettishly, with his hands on his hips, underlining his tiny waist. The feminising power of the earrings combined with the presence of the mirror were making themselves felt.

On this particular occasion, once he had examined himself from a frontal and three-quarter angle, he removed his clothes. He had to change for his lesson anyway, but he did not merely remove his bodice and skirt: he undressed completely, down to the last item, and solemnly scrutinised his body. He was comparing his stripling's physique to the voluptuous body in full bloom which obsessed him.

He was probably thinking that, now that he was a girl, he could realistically aspire to emulate this physical paragon; perhaps it was only a matter of time and the right beauty care. Of course, his hopes did not extend to rivalling his aunt's beauty, but he could visualise the filling out of his breasts and the blossoming of his hips.

For the first time, Fred felt this desire which comes naturally to young girls. The seed which had been sown in him was beginning to grow.

Fred did not see his aunt that afternoon. She went out on an urgent errand during his piano lesson and had made the effort to dress by herself. On any other day, she would have had no qualms in interrupting the lesson, but she thought it best to leave Fred under the influence of the morning's incident until the evening. She thought it preferable to behave like an aloof princess and leave the youth to his musings.

She had barely returned when she heard a knock on the door and to her amazement, Fred entered the room.

She was still in her town clothes, with an expensive hat atop her wavy hair tall patent leather boots and had not had time to remove her long fawn-coloured gloves, she had barely sat down in her boudoir and was about to unseal a letter which had arrived during her absence.

"But Frédérique, I had not yet rung for you."

Fred crossed the threshold and stopped in his tracks; not that he had suddenly become aware of his audacity or that he was paralysed by his aunt's

— Il me prend des envies de vous appeler « maîtresse » (Ch. XI)

upbraiding. Rather, the boudoir filled with flowers and saturated with perfumes was lit with the same blue bulbs as on that memorable evening when he had experienced such terrifying and bizarre happenings.

Madame de Saint-Genest had not changed save for the town outfit which had replaced the diaphanous *negligé;* her arms were still uncovered almost up to her shoulders and their statuesque beauty was eye-catching, but their nudity, immodest in its paleness and delicacy, was concealed beneath the long, shiny and supple gloves which were akin to a taut second skin.

The Baroness was no less beautiful, but she was different, more distant, dour and imposing. The gold pin gleamed at her *décolletage.*

Fred had entered without any purpose, motivated only by his desire to see her again after these long hours spent in solitude and to offer her his menial services. All of a sudden, he was overwhelmed by an irrepressible urge. He crossed the room as if in a trance, made a beeline for this female figure, harmoniously and majestically lit by the blue bulbs, and sank to his knees in front of her, embraced her legs, kissed her knees and, in a state of delirium, uttered fervently,

"Oh aunt! Beautiful aunt! I sometimes get the urge to call you 'Mistress'!"

"I would not find that displeasing."

"Are you in earnest? If I utter that word..."

"You may use it. But in that case, I shall have to call you my slave."

"Am I not your slave already, Mistress?"

He breathed these last words and crumpled in a heap, prostrated himself with his forehead touching the carpet and grabbed hold of one of her patent leather boots with both hands and placed it on his head.

His gesture was so spontaneous, so passionate and unexpected that Léontine could not help quivering to the core. These circumstances egged her on. She had just devised a bold and perverse scheme, the same scheme which she could barely dwell upon when it entered her mind and which would imbue her unabashed gaze with a characteristically warped mistiness.

To be sure, it was a rather shocking idea. But she could afford to take the risk. It was possible now that she sensed that this youth would consider her as his absolute Mistress, and perhaps something more: an idol.

Her mind was made up and she made her decision known: she moved her patent leather foot forward and placed it on the nape of his neck, her disproportionately high heel digging into his flesh.

"Very well, Frédérique! I accept you as my slave but you must promise, swear even, to obey me as a slave, in other words, blindingly and unhesitatingly, conforming yourself scrupulously and religiously to my orders, whatever they may be even (and all the more so) if they are unpleasant."

Every now and then, she imperiously dug her heel into Frédérique's nape to stress the import of her words.

Elle vit son visage transfiguré (Chap. XI).

He repeated the terms of the pledge and concluded with an oath. She added,

"Now you will have to keep your promise. We are bound by a sacred pact whose terms you must never forget."

"How could I ever forget!" he exclaimed, "Just as I shall never forget the blood you drew from my ears."

As she removed her foot, he turned his head so that his cheek rested against the carpet. She saw how the fervour of sacrifice transfigured him; she saw his twinkling earring; she then rose to place her heel on his ear and for an instant, Fred felt the weight of this idolized body and moaned ecstatically as the drop earring into stabbed his flesh.

Chapter Twelve

A Female Slave

The following morning, after Fred had performed his daily duties of helping his aunt out of the bath, wiping her dry, perfuming her and rubbing her down, she changed a detail of the established ritual: as he was taking her kimono off the peg and gathering up her stockings and slippers, she stopped him:

"There is no need. I am not going back to my room just yet. I want to remain here alone for a little while. When I ring, I want you to bring me the mother-of-pearl casket which is on my bedside table."

The unsuspecting Fred left the room assuming that this casket contained rare oils or a manicure set.

Having looked at her graceful nudity with satisfaction in the mirrors, Léontine lay down on the couch which stood in a corner of the bathroom; she covered herself with a fur pelisse which she had brought back from Russia and fell into a *rêverie*.

She was obsessed by a longing to which she was at once on the verge of giving in and evidently struggling to fend off. Twice she was about to press the electric bell switch and twice thought better of it. Feeling impatient, nervous and restless, she tossed and turned on the couch as if trying to find sleep, dangling a leg or stretching an arm. She then lay on her stomach, lifted her bust, and rested on her elbows with her chin on her hands: she had instinctively adopted Cleopatra's pose as is commonly portrayed in art, and her naked body, which conferred a life-like quality to the fur, looked both regal and barbaric.

Finally, for the third time, her finger approached the button: she pressed it and it rang twice as arranged.

Madame de Saint-Genest resumed her pose after pulling the fur coat back onto her loins for it had slipped off when she had extended her arm. She remained still with her eyes fixed on the door. It was not just her pose of a panther lying in wait which likened her to the queen of Egypt; her expression was that of Cleopatra testing the reactions of her slaves to various poisons.

Fred knocked on the door.

Léontine had rung in a resolute manner but she now seemed to waver. Her desire carried such implications that she wondered if it was feasible.

The inner struggle which was raging inside her lasted over a minute; thinking that she hadn't heard, Fred knocked again. This time Léontine thought "To hell with it! Come what may!" with such intensity and force that her words could have been read on her lips and features. Her mind was now fully made up and she uttered "Come in...." in a voice so changed that those two syllables sounded ominous.

Fred was not prepared for the sight that awaited him, visions from antiquity danced before his eyes and the names of all the authoritarian, whimsical *femmes fatales* of history and myth surged up in his mind.

He was enthralled by her facial expression, her gracefully folded arms with one elbow sunk in a cushion and the charming way with which the fur covered her naked body while simultaneously hinting at the supreme harmony of her limbs and the sumptuousness of her full silhouette beneath its suggestive folds.

Léontine uttered her orders in an unusually curt, halting and husky voice:

"Bring me the small key which is on the shelf, go down on one knee and offer me the casket."

He obeyed; she unlocked the casket and took out something wrapped in a silk scarf.

"Good," she continued, "Now go down on both knees next to me and turn around."

She unfolded the scarf which contained a pair of handcuffs.

"Put both hands behind your back," she ordered.

She immediately seized his wrists and snapped the steel clasps shut around them.

She gave him permission to stand and face her; he saw that the fur coat had slipped off and was about to pull it back onto her beautiful naked body but was astounded to hear her order,

"No, leave it, it's fine as it is. Frédérique, kiss my back, kiss me all over, from the nape of my neck to the small of my back."

She did not need to repeat her injunction: he leaned forward, his movements impeded by his chained hands. His kisses were clumsy and hesitant but Léontine had expected this lack of experience and was consequently not at all disappointed. She was totally gripped by the pleasurable sensations afforded by his cool lips touching her voracious skin with a mixture of tenderness, fear and immature emotion.

Fred was too taken aback by the unexpectedness of the incident to note its details; in these bizarre transports of rapture, never experienced before, he had barely any notion of the rapid succession of sensations which made his nerves tingle.

On occasion, the urge to kiss her furtively had crossed his mind when his gaze had been drawn to a patch of white flesh peeping through the lace of her bodice, or to a strip of satin-like skin between her glove and her sleeve; but he never imagined that that very flesh would one day be stretched out, naked and within reach, to welcome his showers of kisses. Besides, his imagination did not extend as far as to depict the strange and intoxicating appeal of fondling someone thus which made his blood boil impetuously, brutally and intermittently and made her loins succumb to delicately light thrills, evidence of gentle, sensuous pleasure.

Deprived of the use of his hands, Fred could only feel intensely through his eyes, nostrils and lips. His gaze gently caressed the contours of her generous flesh, her graceful curves and her dimples, of which he had only caught bedazzled glimpses in the past, while wrapping her in her robe or massaging her with essential oils. His avid nostrils detected with delight the delicately feminine scent exuding from this giant flower of flesh and the traces of exquisite perfumes whose heady and subtle notes he had never smelt so strongly before. His lips, more than his hands ever did, revealed the firm and soft texture of her divine body and the incomparable velvety down of her skin. The myriad of sensations merged to form an indefinable and delicious whole which aroused and pleasured him.

So as to expose as much of her pearly white petals of flesh to the light touch of his lips that were like a crimson butterfly, Léontine turned onto her side. The twin spheres of her buttocks disappeared to be replaced by a round and jutting hip which underlined her slender waist and blended harmoniously with her shapely calves. She now lay on her back: her body was shameless in its beauty and displayed new riches and Fred, in his naive devotion, did not know where to begin.

She had to guide him through this pagan ritual; at first she used words, uttered in a soft and low voice which mitigated her impatience and imperiousness. She indicated a succession of points on her body which quivered with perverse anticipation at the thought of being silently caressed by those cool, crimson lips.

"Kiss me beneath my chin... there... above my breasts... my shoulder... my upper arm... underneath, the blond down... Now this breast... the globe... the nipple... now the other, the dip between them..."

The docile Fred leaned forward and sought these points with his lips, punctuating her every word with a kiss. The discovery of her breasts, thrust out and palpitating, enabled him to become acquainted with the appeal of a stronger taste and his downy cheek brushed against the curves of her proud bosom, which gave them both intense pleasure.

Léontine weakly muttered a few more words which tailed off into a sigh. She then placed her hand onto Fred's head and firmly pushed it down into her secret recesses to fulfil her wordless but urgent concupiscence.

Madame de Saint-Genest tilted back her head in a Bacchante-like pose and writhed with pleasure; her body was virtually naked save for a portion of fur which highlighted her warm and palpitating alabaster skin.

Finally, the imperious hand pushed away the youth who collapsed onto the crumpled fur on the floor. The obedient Fred, impeded by his handcuffs, squatted by the couch. He felt as if he was dreaming, he recalled the delights of the paradise which he had glimpsed without realising that he had only reached its portal.

As for the Baroness, her mysterious smile gave way to a satisfied and triumphant one: she had just sampled the fulfilment of the perverse desire which had haunted her ever since she had become widowed. Fred embodied the female and Sapphic slave which she visualised in her fantasies.

Chapter Thirteen

The Vortex

At one fell swoop, Léontine de Saint-Genest had considerably deepened her ascendancy over young de Montignac; however, she was also aware that there was something risky and even perilous about sensually awakening her nephew and that was why she had hesitated before crossing the Rubicon.

On second thoughts, she had no regrets; she had already behaved in an unnatural way by raising a boy as a girl. She now hoped to completely overthrow nature and believed it was a question of willpower and authority. She was extremely self-willed; as for authority, it had become a despotic hold which she was determined to maintain and even consolidate. The Baroness had reached the stage where all she had to do was reap the fruits of the young shrub which she had so boldly grafted.

From that moment on, a radical change began to operate; its progress was visible each week making Fred's metamorphosis increasingly disturbing. Léontine noted with intense pleasure that his feminisation was not merely superficial, but that in addition to the manners of a girl of his age, he was acquiring girlish personality traits, tastes and even a girl's disposition.

Never before had the influence of clothing been so well illustrated, probably because nobody had applied it with such authority as the Baroness to 'her niece' and female slave.

After strongly expressing his disgust, Fred had developed a taste for female dress and its elegant and futile trappings, because he was now aware that, in this way, he could make himself attractive to his beautiful aunt who had inspired an absolute and passionate affection in him.

First he had become accustomed to his new figure, then he had noted with pleasure how light, opulent fabrics were pleasing to the eye as well as to the touch, how well they hung and how they flattered his young body. He also began to be fond of the trimmings, either sophisticated or more discreet, for he had to admit that they were graceful and elegant when he looked at himself in the mirror.

He would contemplate his mirror-image with increasing frequency and pleasure. At first, he would stop for a moment in front of a mirror to check his appearance or adjust a few details. Later, he would examine himself every time he changed to assess the effect of a different cut or a new hat. Little by little, he got into the habit of looking at himself for no reason, just for pleasure...the pleasure of seeing himself look stylish and dapper, swathed in delicate fabrics with felicitous colour combinations over rustling *lingerie.*

He had acquired the habit and taste for delicate *lingerie* with its slim ribbons and gossamer lace, scented and soft against the skin. He had even learned to accept those Louis heels which had been so painfully uncomfortable at first, but which he now endured because of the excessive arch which they conferred to feet shod in dainty little shoes or tightly-laced tall boots. Perhaps he was also haunted by the memory of imperious tall boots which had weighed down on his neck and which he had kissed with such passion...

Fred was even fond of his corsets, yet their sturdy bones and tight laces were the instruments of a never-ending ordeal. In this respect, Madame de Saint-Genest was on a par with Mrs. Stockley in terms of strictness. Above all else, the Baroness was very intent on her niece Frédérique having a nipped-in waist for a very simple reason: by permanently compressing the waist to an extreme degree, Frédérique would not only have a tiny waist (and this was the main reason), but his hips would be accentuated. By banishing his masculine silhouette, he would definitively be endowed with a female conformation.

The finishing touch to the illusion was the dizzying high heels which, by making him stand on tiptoe, caused his rump to jut out, higher, rounder and exposed for all to see.

Because Fred had become sensitive to the result that had been obtained, he forgot the barbaric methods that had been employed. He would often mince around in front of the mirror, arms akimbo, and was proud of his narrow waist which a man's hands could have encircled. He could not deny that flowery satin corsets decorated with ribbon and lace were aesthetic instruments of torture; he took good care of them and was fond of them. With time, he had warmed to their strange charm and had even come to find this stranglehold strangely pleasurable.

All these items of clothing down to the most frivolous trappings had become so familiar that it never occurred to him that he could wear anything else. It was a miraculous transformation brought about by the ear-piercing episode. He no longer dressed to pander to the whim of a beautiful, perverse and fanciful lady but to fulfil a natural physical need. The only possible garments were feminine and they inevitably went hand in hand with primping, seeking elegant and tasteful finery, and the need to conform to fashion so as to pass unnoticed. That was his greatest fear, the fear that haunts all those who have been through the same experience as Fred.

It was an inescapable training which Fred did not dream of shirking, especially now that the orders were given by his beautiful aunt who had become his imperious Mistress.

In such surroundings, Fred adapted well to his new lifestyle. Léontine eased the transition by giving him a ring which she slipped onto his finger on his name day and a bracelet which she made him wear on the anniversary of his ear-piercing and which he would come to wear with as much pleasure as the long and supple *glacé* kid gloves which he donned when he went out with the Baroness.

She made him lead a girl's life while she waited for his hair to grow long enough to be pinned up into a bun which would sanction him as a woman and which would entitle her to treat him completely like a girl. On that day, Madame de Saint-Genest would shower him with jewels, would teach him how to powder his face and how to use discreet make-up to go out.

Thus his silhouette would no longer cut an equivocal figure, the moral conversion would equal the physical one. Only then would Léontine introduce her niece to high society, take him out with her to visit friends or to the ball. The Baroness envisaged these possibilities insofar as she was certain that, on the strength of the training which she was imposing on 'her niece' in the realms of her private service and sensual whims, she would rule, unrivalled, over his heart and senses despite the onset of puberty which would make him a man unbeknownst to all.

Léontine knew — she was well-informed — that one had to allow two and a half to three years for an adolescent boy's hair to attain the length of a woman's hair. Well, she would be patient until then. As it was, Fred's hairdo was not far removed from the bobs of many women and girls. But that was not good enough for Léontine and she would have to wait patiently for that time to come.

Her patience was boundless for Fred was not the only one to be trapped in a vortex: she had enjoyed Fred's first caresses with such acute pleasure that she repeated the experience with slight variations in time, setting and dress.

Her lust sometimes flared up without warning and the female slave would imperiously be summoned to become a caress-dispenser, a kissing-machine, obeying orders, guided by words or gestures.

She would be in bed, warm and fragrant, dressed in transparent lawn or in evening wear, or swathed in rustling and sumptuous fabrics, elegantly shod, luxuriously gloved or idly recumbent on a *chaise-longue* in the loose folds of a trimmed and diaphanous *négligé* or even in the splendour of a ballgown and flashing gems, what she happened to be wearing was of no importance. She desired, she summoned, she gave orders and was obeyed.

She always took the precaution of handcuffing Fred or binding his hands securely. This was not a malicious gesture, but one of caution, to forestall a potentially disagreeable surprise.

Besides, Léontine may well have been perverse, whimsical and authoritarian, but she was never cruel towards Fred. She was severe merely because it was in her nature and more specifically part of her lifestyle, but she never treated him badly. If she was not satisfied with his services at table or in the bedroom, if he ignored a word of advice regarding his dress, if he was lazy, neglectful or moody, she would whip him but never made him bleed. Similarly, each time she required a sexual favour, she would tie his hands behind his back or, if the handcuffs were not within reach, she would resort to any sort of tie: a cord, a lace, a rope or a silk sash which she tied as tightly as possible to prevent him from taking on a more active role, but she never hurt him more than was necessary.

Chapter Fourteen

An English Education

One day when they were out walking, Fred and his aunt met Mrs. Stockley who was delighted to see her former Sainte-Brigitte pupil got up in this way.

The strict schoolmistress thought Mademoiselle de Montignac looked extremely well and complimented her on her earrings, her shoes and her gloves; she was evidently glad to see that her bizarre enterprise had survived and had even been carried through to a successful conclusion by Madame de Saint-Genest. The encounter was not as satisfying to Fred and brought back woeful memories of the months spent under Mrs. Stockley's rule: the torments that he had had to endure in that mixed boarding-school where female uniform had been inflicted on him came flooding back. He had unpleasant memories of violent scenes where he had been forced to wear girls' clothing, the terrible discipline of overly constricting boots and corsets which squeezed him so tightly as to all but suffocate him. He remembered the punishments used to counter the slightest infringement of the rules, the public humiliations, the heavy and complex chains, the merciless whippings; he remembered the torments intended to check rebellion and attempts to escape and the ghastly nights spent in the dungeon, fettered to the wall.[5] Mrs. Stockley wished to question the Baroness who was only too glad to converse with her. The two ladies entered a tea-room and consigned Fred to the back of the room and to the furthest possible table so as to converse freely.

The headmistress and the socialite exchanged their views on the educational methods which were being applied to Fred and which Mrs. Stockley thought unrivalled to tame unruly young boys whom no other disciplinary method could overcome. She delivered a lecture on the benefits of earrings and their extraordinary influence. The pair discussed the various avatars which lead to perfection: Fred was getting close, but had not yet attained it.

Mrs. Stockley, who was extremely experienced, held forth at length on the subject and her interlocutor found it all most interesting. She clinched the topic by claiming that boys dressed and raised as girls were more widespread than is commonly believed; she had obtained this information from a doctor. These anomalies are not normally detectable given that, once they have fully adapted to their new lifestyle, these male crossdressers give a plausible illusion of femininity.

"For instance, have you ever noticed that some

---

[5] This alludes to *Fred* by Don Brennus Aléra, published by Select-Bibliothèque.

men in elevated circles, even aristocrats, bear scars on their ear-lobes? This proves that they were raised as girls and that their ears were pierced. And it is also very probable that some of these men never revert to men's clothing. They spend their entire life in female harness and they do not arouse our suspicions for they have adapted so well to their feminine lifestyle and are so at ease in women's clothes and trappings; of course, they would never make the mistake of omitting such an exclusively feminine detail as ear-pendants: for earrings complement a face accentuated by the careful use of make-up and long, dyed hair."

"We have not yet reached that stage with Frédérique, but that will come." concluded the Baroness taking leave of Mrs. Stockley and calling 'her niece'.

Fred was somewhat distressed by this unexpected resurfacing of a past which he abhorred. Yet, when Mrs. Stockley, looking strict and severe in a well-cut black dress, lifted her foot and revealed her leg to get into her car, Fred could not help but stare at this woman whom Fate had chosen as his Mistress and whose oppressive and formidable rule had been instrumental in promoting his present state of subjection.

Léontine intercepted his gaze and regretted the encounter because it had reawakened too many of her nephew's memories. She thought it of paramount importance to provoke some sort of reaction in him, to win him back completely, and more crucially, if she wanted her work to be perfect and lasting, to obliterate all traces of his past.

At the Stockley school, he had been raised like all the other boys: he wore girls' clothes only because he was continually and ruthlessly pressured into doing so; if Léontine's plan was to come to fruition, it was crucial that such memories should be annihilated, even in his dreams.

These reflections spurred Madame de Saint-Genest into returning home as quickly as possible. Besides, she felt the need to be alone with her female slave who had become indispensable in calming her sensual demands.

She took 'her niece' straight up to her room and with her help, removed only her hat and dress; wearing only her corset and petticoat and having not had time to remove her long shimmering gloves, she took the silk belt from one of her dressing gowns and approached Fred who had only taken off his hat. She grabbed his frail arms, joined them together behind his back and tied his wrists firmly. She then lay down onto a comfortably padded *chaise-longue*, panting, with crazed eyes and a heaving bosom and exposed with magnificent immodesty her round, slightly plump neck, burnished like a slim ivory pillar, her gently sloping shoulders and her marmoreal breasts with their erect pink nipples. In her haste, she had adopted a pose which, had Fred not been tied up, would have suggested a surrender, a voluptuous capitulation; the evocative disorderliness of her underwear revealed her legs covered in silk and a wide band of smooth, white satin flesh between the stocking and the pastel-coloured suspender.

She gave the order which Fred knew so well: "Kiss me Frédérique!... Kiss everything you see..."

He leaned forward, his gloved hands imprisoned by the silk belt which had been hastily tied and which cut into his wrists; he began to cover her body with kisses which were each time more and more knowing as a result of his experience and his desire to please.

After a few moments, his Mistress's gloved hand pressed down on her slave's head and her desire had the upper hand over his random caresses.

Suddenly Fred stood upright, rigid with fear: after a violent spasm which had made her writhe and moan, Léontine had stopped moving. She turned cold and her eyes rolled upwards. He panicked at the sight of this body, cold and pale as marble, whose bosom was no longer heaving and whose heart seemed to have stopped.

She remained prostrate for quite some time; his hands being tied, Fred could not come to her assistance in any way. The thought of calling someone crossed his mind but in order to do that, he had to get out of the room. He thought of picking up an object between his teeth to press the electric bell switch; but the bolt would have to be drawn. Above all, Fred resented having to divulge his bound hands to the domestic staff.

At last, her bosom twitched, her eyes came back to life and she slowly came round.

Chapter Fifteen

The Final Clinch

Léontine questioned Fred about the length and symptoms of her fainting fit and thought it necessary to consult her physician. He examined her and decided to be direct: she had a heart complaint and could expire at any minute. He made it very clear that she had to avoid strong emotions, especially if they were pleasurable.

Léontine had barely stepped out of the doctor's surgery that she exclaimed the same words as on the day when, naked under her fur, she had summoned Fred to her bathroom:

"To hell with it!" However, she immediately thought of making the necessary arrangements in the event of the outcome of which she had been forewarned. She began to seek a substitute Mistress for Fred.

She deemed that a boy's happiness lay in an English education pushed to the extreme she had reached with Fred; she was certain that, to be perfectly happy, a boy had to play the role that Fred had been allotted in her house.

Particularly in Fred's case, she was firmly convinced that for her thoroughly feminised nephew, there was no other life, let alone a happy one, aside from his dual existence of a well-trained maidservant and a docile page trained to perform amorous duties.

It was patent that Mrs. Stockley's one-time pupil, being a victim of an extreme lifestyle, was totally unprepared for the hardships of life and had even become incapable of leading a normal existence; his education needed a complete reworking, it was difficult to predict whether a return to nature was still possible or if a readaptation could succeed; perhaps the feminine stamp was too deeply ingrained to be deleted and it was highly probable that if Fred was forced to reintegrate a boy's condition, he would be ill-at-ease and even miserable.

Léontine pressed the argument further: she was sincerely convinced that the habits which she had inculcated in Fred had now become so precious to him that he could not live without them. Her opinion was bolstered by observing him continually; she had noticed Fred's increasing vanity, his concern for elegance, his sound taste for furbelows and his interest in housework, needlework and all those feminine occupations and recreations. She had also correctly noted how moved and fervently devoted he was when his trembling lips approached her queenly and shameless nakedness. He was still too young to experience a voluptuous frenzy during these dangerous games, a frenzy which would no doubt manifest itself in him any day, but for the time being, he was already moved to the core: the pleasure which he experienced was irrational and sedate, but it was pleasure nonetheless.

Now that Léontine knew she had only a short time to live, her new goal was to find the woman who would be worthy of continuing her work.

It would prove arduous, for Madame de Saint-Genest required many qualities: the prospective woman would have to be pretty, elegant, intelligent, with allure and prestige, and last but not least, she would have to have certain tendencies. Finally, she would also have to be wealthy so as to be independent and accustomed to the comfortable existence led by Fred. She would have to be broad-minded so as not to baulk at the improper aspect of the situation and single-mindedly impervious to the probable drawbacks and responsibilities which she would have to shoulder and she would need the utmost willpower; to cap it all, it would be perfect if she was an aristocrat with a title. This last condition was her least essential concern; Léontine would have been content with a woman of common birth provided she was refined and, for want of birth and rank, possessed a patrician's soul and tastes. But Léontine would not compromise regarding the two pivotal qualities: a strong will and boundless energy.

With such requirements in mind, the search could only be long and arduous, and indeed it was.

The Baroness did the rounds of her connections and decreed that none of her friends were qualified for the job. Even the more daring ones would have jibed at the audacity of the idea. More to the point:

how did one seek them out?

That was the main hurdle: to make people understand that this was a situation with a difference, an anomaly. It was very delicate to put across, perhaps it would be easier to go into more detail once she had tracked down a woman offering the necessary abilities and dose of perversity. But until then, she would need unlimited shrewdness and circumspection.

At first, Léontine could see but one solution: the small advertisements. She placed a few in appropriate newspapers and worded them differently each time, in vague and cryptic terms so as to provoke replies from which she could draw inferences. She merely made it clear that she was targeting a domineering and awe-inspiring woman with an imposing physique and a taste for domination and who had to have a pastime that was relevant to her abilities.

She received a number of disappointing responses from professionals who had a flair for vice and offered their services merely in exchange for easy gain. Léontine rejected them and after this first selection, trawled through a vast number of letters written by energetic women who were drawn to the underlying risk; she answered them and on the basis of their second letters proceeded to another selection. As the correspondence went on, her selection narrowed down more and more. The Baroness combed out disturbingly unhinged candidates and debased social outcasts and finally cast the entire bundle into the fire.

Undaunted, she repeated the experiment and

retained two letters which stood out from the rest. The enclosed photographs inspired her with confidence and, without divulging her secret, she started up a correspondence which would enable her to closely examine these two women. She eventually ended her correspondence with one of them who seemed to possess a cruel streak. As for the other, one particular sentence had made Léontine doubt her qualities, namely her energy, and so the Baroness did not follow up the correspondence.

These fruitless attempts had taken a few months during which time Madame de Saint-Genest had not forgone her perverse desires: she frequently used her slave to obtain the Sapphic pleasures that she longed for and which Fred gave her with increasing skill. Yet, when Léontine saw that her first attempts had failed, she reduced the frequency of the sessions and, above all, did not give in to her sexual demands. She did not wish to risk an accident before ensuring 'her niece's' future.

On the other hand, she pursued her quest with unrelenting energy. Reverting to her initial idea of scouring her acquaintances, she increased her social circle, carefully enquired about the more eccentric women, young widows or recently divorced ladies whom gossips credited with an iron will and refined tastes, especially if the latter seemed rather peculiar.

On more than one occasion, a glimmer of hope was dashed by disappointment and she never trusted anyone enough to disclose her jealously guarded secret.

The thought of this ideal woman occupied her every waking hour and sometimes in shops, restaurants or at the theatre she would go up to beautiful strangers who had a lofty appearance, a volontary chin and a steady gaze or if she overheard a remark or observed a gesture which had drawn her attention. She believed that in such a quest, perhaps fate was the best guide, or rather fate combined with her intuition and her passionate desire to find someone at all costs.

And indeed, she very nearly did. She met women with all the desirable qualities and answering all the necessary criteria. But there were material obstacles, a lover, a husband or children, which ruled out the possibility of independence.

To succeed, she delved into the resources of her imagination. She even went so far as to organise, through a third party, an art exhibition comprising paintings, etchings and sculptures which were a little *risqué* and especially bizarre, representing scenes of slavery and equivocally androgynous cross-dressing, or shows where pleasure was sought by way of strange and disconcerting refinements. Lying in wait in the exhibition hall, poised to pounce on her prey, she scrutinised faces, eavesdropped on conversations and strove to seek out, of those women whose attention was drawn and held by the more peculiar exhibits, the ones who would pass muster.

In the wake of this exhibition, she set about following three trails which she gave up one after the other having realised that these women were profoundly depraved and would have got Fred addicted to ether, morphine or opium.

Léontine continued to let herself be caressed by Fred but without ever granting him anything. She could see that she was not meeting her deadline and restrained her pleasure accordingly when she isolated herself from the outside world with her docile slave for company, bound as tightly as ever. Although she avoided excess, the ritual was jeopardising her health; she experienced dizzy spells, vertigo and disturbing sensations which were so many warning signs, so she threw herself headlong into the pursuit of this elusive fantasy of finding a new guardian for Frédérique.

There was something very moving and even magnificent about her passionate and obsessional quest for this woman who would supplant her after her death.

This obsession did not contain one iota of sadism: Léontine was not seeking satisfaction beyond the grave in the certainty that after her death, someone would be there to molest the boy. On the contrary, she rejected cruel females who, out of spitefulness, would have made his life a misery with the same determination as the perverts would have degraded him. It was for his future happiness (which had to equal his past happiness) that she wanted to be sure that her death would not deprive her nephew of the strict discipline, feminine lifestyle and peculiar inclinations which she believed played a central role in his happiness. Fred was destined to a life of servitude in petticoats under the heel of a beautiful authoritarian woman. She had forged gold bonds for her slave, chains of which he had become fond and which would never be broken.

The threat of death which hung over her imbued her enterprise with true greatness; her striving will was feverishly stimulated as a result. Although she did her best to hasten the ineluctable outcome, she *knew* that it would not happen too soon because she *had* to provide for Fred first and hand him over to a Mistress who was capable of ruling him, of imparting to him the joys of waiting upon a woman, in other words, a woman who was worthy of succeeding to the Baroness Léontine de Saint-Genest.

And so the quest continued, becoming more and more dogged but remaining fruitless.

Léontine grew tired and finally resorted to visiting the Canoness, an extraordinary slave-dealer who had founded a luxury slave emporium in Paris.

Léontine had first got wind of her in a conversation overheard at a ball and which referred to a woman who was a guest's slave and who had been purchased from the Canoness. The snippet of conversation had aroused Léontine's curiosity and she wished to meet this mythical adventuress.

She told herself that if Madame de Mareuil sold high-class slaves, then her clientele must be composed of an *élite* of dominatrices among whom she would find the ideal woman who would become a suitable Mistress for Fred.

The Baroness succeeded in making contact with this pirate in custom-made dresses who recruited her prey from every background but especially from the aristocracy, the stage and the cosmopolitan *salons* of the capital. But the Canoness, with her habitual wariness, carefully avoided ushering Léontine into her mysterious establishment, which was very well organised and well-guarded, was situated in a safe Parisian neighbourhood, and so they met in the reading-room of a department store instead.[6]

Léontine had barely spoken before the Canoness was riveted and wanted to find out more. She steered the conversation in such a way as to draw out more detail from the Baroness. Léontine found herself saying more than she had ever written, mentioning Fred and certain particulars; she then gave a description of the physical gifts, qualities and personality traits which she required in the ideal woman. The Canoness assured her that several of her clients possessed these characteristics, especially one of them.

Madame de Saint-Genest's instinct instantly alerted her; she was suddenly scared of this woman of prey who had succeeded in reinstating slavery in the twentieth century and was exploiting the freedom of her contemporaries. She sensed that she was going to become the victim of a sinister plot, that this trafficker would put her in touch with one of her accommodating clients, perhaps one of her purveyors or even one of her slaves. Thanks to this go-between, Fred would fall into the powerful hands of the Canoness whose only concern would be to

---

[6] The Canoness is the enigmatic and colourful character featured in other novels by Don Brennus Aléra. The main titles are *The Canoness*, *The Gloved Slave* and *Slave Markets* all published by Select-Bibliothèque.

make a huge profit by selling him to the highest bidder, whoever they may be.

Indeed, Madame de Mareuil was capable of such a thing. Léontine even feared a more daring plot: having caught this woman of prey sizing her up with the gaze of a shady horse-dealer, she wondered if the Canoness was not thinking of compromising her completely so as to have an advantage over her and blackmail her for her beauty and her freedom. Léontine was not mistaken. The Canoness, who was well-informed and depraved through and through, had read between the lines and wondered if it was possible to reduce this admirable woman to slavery, and if so, how much the Baroness Saint-Genest would fetch, naked and in fetters, in a clandestine showroom.

Léontine suddenly found this empress of decadence supremely unpleasant and disquieting with her round and heavily made-up face, her cruelty and perversity concealed beneath mock respectability and her claims to society life. Totally aghast, Léontine curtailed her visit and took leave.

Her plans had ground to a halt. Death was getting ever closer, that Léontine could tell from her symptoms.

All in all, these attempts had taken up an entire year. Fred was fifteen years old. His hair reached his shoulder blades. He was now a young lady whose sex was unquestionable. The pleasure which, tightly bound, he expertly gave his Mistress with his submissive lips was becoming ever deeper. Léontine knew that she was committing suicide, but before she died, she wanted to finalise her arrangements.

And that is exactly what she did.

She had heard of a Hungarian Countess recently estranged from her husband, young, tall, slim, dark-haired and breathtakingly beautiful, boldly elegant, very imperious, famous for her whims and fancies, her loathing of banality, her penchant for the most extravagant and unusual situations and for the most hazardous adventures. Madame de Saint-Genest established an epistolary relationship with her.

The correspondence was regular, lengthy and became less and less restrained. Léontine would dissect each letter sentence by sentence and her analysis — the most profound she had ever undertaken — would each time reveal new grounds for satisfaction. The photograph completed the idyllic picture for it promised a woman of strange and disturbing beauty.

What is more, the countess was rich. This detail had become of secondary importance in Léontine's priorities because, all things considered, Fred had a private income and there was also her own means.

As soon as she had become well-acquainted with the Countess' character, tastes, qualities and shortcomings, Léontine made overtures which hazily revealed her intentions. The foreign lady replied in such a way as to make the Baroness feel that she would be fully understood and her mind was firmly made up.[7]

From that moment, Madame de Saint-Genest

calmly and meticulously made her final provisions. She consulted a few experts with utter seriousness and in great depth and attempted to bend the law in favour of the supreme plan which was so close to her heart. When she had weighed the pros and cons, thought everything out and planned everything down to the smallest details, she made all the necessary arrangements in a perfectly legal and unimpeachable manner which would guarantee the execution of her wishes. She settled everything so that, in the event of her death, Frédérique the slave would only change hands and would truly be *bequeathed* to the Hungarian Countess as if he were a piece of furniture or a jewel. Léontine could die in peace.

Three days after carrying out the final formalities, the Baroness Saint-Genest passed away suddenly, comforted by the thought that she had forever riveted the gold chain which made Fred de Montignac an eternal prisoner of womankind.

In the mortuary chapel filled with flowers and light, Fred, pale in his black mourning *crêpe* was weeping beneath his black veil. Beside him, in the casket which contained his handcuffs was a sealed envelope bearing a coat of arms which contained the secret of his destiny.

[7] The reader may be interested to know that it was I who unwittingly caused this choice. I happened to describe a few typical characteristics of this Hungarian Countess in the presence of Madame de Saint-Genest. Madame de Saint-Genest did not come and see me: because she had confided in me, she felt that I would divine the reason behind her questions and preferred to avoid a refusal. She discovered the identity and the address of this Countess all by herself, but to make contact with her, she used my name without my knowledge.

Frédérique

To be continued ...
in
*Frida: The True Story of a Young Man
Becoming a Young Woman*

... Coming soon from Delectus

DELECTUS

"The world's premiere publisher of classic erotica." *Bizarre.*

DELECTUS HARDBACKS

THE PETTICOAT DOMINANT OR, WOMAN'S REVENGE

An insolent aristocratic youth, Charles, makes an unwelcome, though not initially discouraged pass at his voluptuous tutoress Laura. In disgust at this transgression she sends Charles to stay with her cousin Diane d'Erebe, in a large country house inhabited by a coterie of governesses. They put him through a strict regime of corrective training, involving urolagnia, and enforced feminisation; dressing him in corsets and petticoats to rectify his unruly character.

Written under a pseudonym, by London lawyer Stanislas De Rhodes, and first published in 1898 by Leonard Smithers' *Erotica Biblion Society*, Delectus have reset the original into a new edition.

"Frantic...breathless...spicy...restating the publisher's place at the top of the erotic heap." *Divinity*. "A great classic of fetish erotica...A marvellous period piece." *Bizarre*. "Delicious..." *Sydney Morning Herald*.

Delectus 1994 hbk 120p. £19.95

FRIDA: THE TRUE STORY OF A YOUNG MAN BECOMING A YOUNG WOMAN - DON BRENNUS ALERA

The stunning sequel to the book you have just read follows our hero to a new Mistress and new experience Translated by Valerie Orpen and due to be published in 1999.

THE MISTRESS & THE SLAVE

A Parisian gentleman of position and wealth begins a romantic liaison with Anna, a poor, but voluptuous young woman, and falls wholly under her spell. Her power is complete. There is no doubt or hesitation in its wielding. Completely enchanted we watch George descend into his own private oblivion. He is powerless to resist. The greater the cruelty and humiliation, the deeper his submission becomes. His passion to obey becomes his obsession. The perversity of Anna's nature with it's absolute domination over him, ultimately culminates in a tragic ending.

"But, my child, you don't seem to understand what a Mistress is. For instance: your child your favourite daughter, might be dying and I should send you to the Bastille to get me a twopenny trinket. You would go, you would obey! Do you understand?" - "Yes!" he murmured, so pale and troubled that he could scarcely breathe. "And you will do everything I wish?" - "Everything, darling Mistress! Everything! I swear it to you!"

"Sordid...gripping...extreme...highly unhygienic fun." *Fiesta*. "Anna is one hell of a woman, and The Mistress and the Slave is an S/M classic." *Screw*. "Another delectabl classic for collectors of decadent erotica...it possesses an elegance rare in today's erotic prose." *Desir* "Compelling...another gem to excite." *KPPT*. "Sadistic & unpleasant." *Headpress*. "Powerful and explicit *Lust*. "Imperious humiliation." *Fetish Times*.

Delectus 1995 hbk in d/j 160p. £19.9

A GUIDE TO THE CORRECTION OF YOUNG GENTLEMEN - "A LADY"

The ultimate guide to Victorian domestic discipline, lost since all previously known copies were destroyed by court order nearly seventy years ago.

"Her careful arrangement of subordinate clauses is truly masterful." *The Daily Telegraph.* "I rate this book as near biblical in stature." *The Naughty Victorian.* "The lady guides us through the corporal stages with uncommon relish and an experienced eye to detail...An absolute gem of a book." *Zeitgeist.* "An exhaustive guide to female domination." *Divinity.* "Essential reading for the modern enthusiast with taste." *Skin Two.*

Delectus 1994 hbk with a superb cover by Sardax 140p with over 30 illustrations. £19.95

PAINFUL PLEASURES

A fascinating miscellany of relentless spankomania comprising letters, short stories and true accounts. Originally published in New York 1931, Delectus have produced a complete facsimile complemented by the beautiful art deco line illustrations vividly depicting punishment scenes from the book.

Both genders end up with smarting backsides in such stories as *The Adventures of Miss Flossie Evans,* and, probably the best spanking story ever written, *Discipline at Parame,* in which a stern and uncompromising disciplinarian brings her two cousins Elsie and Peter to meek and prompt obedience. An earlier section contains eight genuine letters and an essay discussing the various merits of discipline and corporal punishment.

The writing is of the highest quality putting many of the current mass market publishers to shame, and Delectus into a class of its own.

"An extraordinary collection...as fresh and appealing now as in its days of shady celebrity...especially brilliant...another masterpiece...a collectors treasure." *Paddles.* "An American S/M classic." *The Bookseller.* "Sophisticated...handsomely printed... classy illustrations...beautifully bound." *Desire.* "For anyone who delights in the roguish elegance of Victorian erotica...this book is highly recommended." *Lust.* "A cracking good read." *Mayfair.*

Delectus 1995 hbk in imperial purple d/j 272p. £19.95

THE ROMANCE OF CHASTISEMENT; OR, REVELATIONS OF SCHOOL AND BEDROOM - "AN EXPERT"

The *Romance* is filled with saucy tales comprising headmistresses taking a birch to the bare backsides of schoolgirls, women whipping each other, men spanking women, an aunt whipping her nephew and further painful pleasures.

Delectus have produced a complete facsimile of the rare 1888 edition of this renowned and elegant collection of verse, prose and anecdotes on the subject of the Victorian English gentleman's favourite vice: Flagellation!

"One of the all time flagellation classics." *The Literary Review*, "In an entirely different class...A chronicle of punishment, pain and pleasure." *Time Out.* "A classic of Victorian vice." *Forum*, "A very intense volume...a potent, single-minded ode to flagellation." *Divinity*, "A delightful book of awesome contemporary significance...beautifully written." *Daily Telegraph.* "Stylishly produced and lovingly illuminated with elegant graphics and pictures...written in a style which is charming, archaic and packed with fine detail." *The Redeemer.*

Delectus 1993 hbk 160p. £19.95

MODERN SLAVES - CLAIRE WILLOWS

From the same publishers as *Painful Pleasures* and *The Strap Returns*, this superb novel, from 1931, relates the story of young Laura who is sent from New York to stay with her uncle in England. However, through a supposed case of mistaken identity, she finds herself handed over to a mysterious woman, who had engineered the situation to suit her own ends. She is whisked away to an all female house of correction, Mrs. Wharton's Training School, in darkest Thurso in the far north of Scotland. Here she undergoes a strict daily regime under the stern tutelage of various strict disciplinarians, before being sold to Lady Manville as a maid and slave. There she joins two other girls and a page boy, William, all of whom Lady Manville disciplines with a unique and whole hearted fervour.

Delectus have produced a beautiful facsimile reproduction of the original Gargoyle edition from the golden decade of American erotica, including 10 superb art-deco style line drawings explicitly depicting scenes from the novel.

"Another classic from Delectus." *Eros*. "Another gem... beautifully illustrated." *Paddles*.

Delectus 1995 hbk in imperial purple d/j 288p. £19.9

THE STRAP RETURNS: NEW NOTES ON FLAGELLATION

This remarkable book contains letters, authentic episodes and short stories including *A Governess Lectures on the Art of Spanking*, *A Woman's Revenge* and *The Price of a Silk Handkerchief or, How a Guilty Valet was Rewarded*, along with decorations and six full page line drawings by Vladimir Alexandre Karenin.

A superb and attractive facsimile of an anthology from 1933, originally issued in New York by the same publishers of two other Delectus titles, *Painful Pleasures* and *Modern Slaves*.

Delectus 1998 hbk (Due Oct.) 220p. £19.95

WHITE STAINS - "ANAIS NIN & FRIENDS"

In *Alice* a couple spying on a another couple screwing in a public park become involved in a steamy group sex scene. In *Florence*, a New York office girl enjoys sex for the first time...sleeping with two men in quick succession! In *Memories* a man recounts his youth and his teenage initiation into sex by a variety of older women.

This collection of six sensual, yet explicit short stories is thought to have been written for an Oklahoma oil millionaire, Roy M. Johnson. Anais Nin is said to have paid a dollar per page to produce typescripts of explicit erotica for his own private amusement.

This facsimile reproduction also contains an explicit sex manual, *Love's Cyclopaedia*, originally published with the stories. The introduction by Dr. C.J. Scheiner tells the story of the books first clandestine edition by New York publisher Samuel Roth during the 1940s and, all the evidence for attributing this anonymous wc to Anais Nin.

"Extremely filthy...groin gripping...rampant...a great ensemble of work." *Forum*. "The highly erotic stor leave nothing to the imagination." *Marquis*. "Unique...torrid...blood stirring...a masterpiece." *Redempt* (Canada). "Beautifully written." *Lust*. "Yet another fascinating title." *Studio*. "Sensuous sexual fantas *Sydney Morning Herald*. "Class stuff." *Loaded*. "A book that the serious collector cannot be witho *Galaxy*. Delectus 1995 hbk in d/j 220p. £19

WHITE WOMEN SLAVES - DON BRENNUS ALERA

in America's deep south in the years just preceding the American Civil
r this book follows the life of Englishman, Lord Ascot, and his associates
he State of Louisiana. Originally published by The Select Bibliotheque
910 and written by the prolific author of *Frédérique*, this book contains
eight original illustrations.

Delectus 1999 hbk 270p. £19.95

MASOCHISM IN AMERICA OR, MEMOIRS OF A VICTIM OF FEMINISM - PIERRE MAC ORLAN

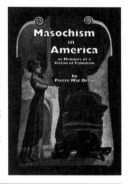

rench erotic classic, first published in the 1920s, by surrealist, war hero,
renowned popular thriller writer, Pierre Mac Orlan, this crafted collection
erotic vignettes provides a male masochistic odyssey through America.

nslated, for the first time into English by Alexis Lykiard, and including
J. Sonrel illustrations from the French original.

Delectus 1999 hbk 200p. £19.95

DELECTUS PAPERBACKS

SCREAM, MY DARLING, SCREAM! - ANGELA PEARSON

stunning short stories of lust, merciless female dominance and cowering
le submission.

ilty of Objectionable Behaviour features a merchant seaman who is
uced by the hypnotic beauty of a beautiful Arabian girl. The mysterious
nger is revealed to be the Sheikh's daughter and a Princess to boot. He is
ested and swiftly passed into the custody of the Princess Makasile who,
h her assistant, the sadistic Salome, keeps him as her personal slave.

the title story a couple travelling through Europe discover a bizarre
lerground nightclub in Marseilles. The more intoxicated they get, the
re extreme their behaviour becomes, culminating with a most unusual
aret in which they become the most willing participants.

ese classic stories are by the author of another Delectus bestseller *There's
/hip in My Valise*.

*e put her free hand to her breasts beneath her robe. "I love to hear you cry out," she gasped. "Scream!
eam your head off! Nobody will hear ." She struck again... and again... and again...'*

ie extreme activities make New York's fetish clubs look like an English tea dance. Refreshing...literate,
lligent and beautifully produced." *New York Free Press.*

Delectus 1998 pbk 200p. £9.99

THERE'S A WHIP IN MY VALISE - GRETA X

Meet four merciless women plus one nymphomaniac. Their wanton passions leave a trail of whipped and buggered men throughout Europe. These rubber clad ladies lust for blood, and it flies! Poor Per Petersen has no idea how far these femmes fatales will take him until they descend on his home to give him a night to remember!

"My helpless whipping boy. He has to do whatever I tell him. He has to come obediently for his regular whippings. He has to do whatever terrible things I order him to do. And he cringes under my whip like a thrashed dog. He is absolutely under my thumb, isn't he? He daren't object, he daren't refuse me anything, and he daren't run away, dare he? He is totally in my power, isn't he?"

"Wild!" *Eros.* "Top stuff!" *Loaded.* "Awesome...juicy..." *Forum.* "If you like your domination heavy this may be the book for you." *Desire.* "For men who like their women dominant and beautiful." *Paddles.*

Delectus 1995 pbk 200p. £

THE WHIPPING CLUB - ANGELA PEARSON

Ms. Pearson's perverse imagination is once again given full reign in this superb novel about a select club of young women dedicated dedicated to extreme female domination. Their bizarre activities culminate in a wild party at Buckley Manor where anything and everything goes.

"Bill continued to beg for mercy, his voice now raised to a piteous scream. Jane gave no mercy, felt no pity. She lashed wildly, constantly shoving him back to the floor with her foot when he attempted to rise."

Delectus 1998 pbk 258p. £9.99

THE WHIPPING POST - ANGELA PEARSON

The superb sequel to *The Whipping Club* follows Rodney Pearce and o members on to further adventures in relentless female domination.

Delectus 1998 pbk 256p. £

---

120 DAYS OF SODOM - ADAPTED FOR THE STAGE BY NICK HEDGES FROM THE NOVEL BY THE MARQUIS DE SADE

Four libertines take a group of young men and women together with four old whores to a deserted castle. Here they engage in a four month marathon of cruelty, debasement, and debauchery.

This award winning play features photographs from the London production and a revealing interview with the director.

"A bizarre pantomime of depravity that makes the Kama Sutra read like a guide to personal hygiene." *What's On.* "If you missed the play, you definitely need to get the book." *Rouge.* "Unforgettable...their most talked about publication so far." *Risque.*

Delectus 1991 pbk 112p. £